stride's
summer

Jenni Overend

stride's summer

ALLEN&UNWIN

First published in 2007

Allen & Unwin
83 Alexander Street
Crows Nest NSW 2065
Australia
Phone: (61 2) 8425 0100
Fax: (61 2) 9906 2218
Email: info@allenandunwin.com
Web: www.allenandunwin.com

National Library of Australia
Cataloguing-in-Publication entry:
Overend, Jenni, 1956 –.
Stride's summer.
ISBN 978 1 74114 084 2 (pbk).
I. Title.
A823.3

Design by Ellie Exarchos
Cover images: Dave Watts/ANTPhoto.com (Sulphur-Crested Cockatoo)
& Burke/Triolo Productions / BrandX / Corbis ([Boy] with surboard)
Set in 10/14.5pt Electra by Midland Typesetters, Australia
Printed in Australia by McPherson's Printing Group

To my mother whose childhood was brightened
by a sulphur-crested cockatoo

1 Mayday

Rain fell in sheets from an iron sky as the procession of cars crawled along the streaming road. Stride watched from the window of the hearse, his suit tight across his shoulders. He tried to imagine it was a wetsuit, and the sound of the car's engine was the roar of breaking waves and the blur in his eyes was salt spray on an offshore breeze. But the hired jacket didn't sit snug like his wetsuit, the drone of the car was nothing like the surge of waves, and the sting in his eyes was because behind him, in a coffin beneath a huge bouquet of flowers, lay his father.

The phone call had come in the middle of the night. Stride struggled to wake out of a deep sleep that clung to him from somewhere dark and green. His thoughts were shadowy and confused. He reached for the light. The ringing in the next room had stopped. The wind howled, tearing at the corners of the house. And above it he heard his mother's voice: 'Yes . . . yes . . . I'm his wife, Caroline. I understand . . . Yes . . . but . . . of course . . . of course . . . I'll be here . . . by the phone . . . Is there anything . . . Of course not . . . No, I'll be here . . . Please call if there's any news, anything at all . . .'

Stride slid out of bed. He stood in the doorway, watching his mother outlined in the glow from the open fire. She had her back to him, her head down, her long fair hair swept to one side. The telephone was hanging loosely from her hand.

'Mum?' Stride's voice was low and throbbed in his throat. 'Mum?'

She turned, eyes wide, in the half light.

'Oh, Stride, you're awake . . .'

'What is it?'

She didn't answer.

He stepped forward and grabbed the phone. 'What is it?' he repeated. He held the receiver to his ear. Beep, beep, beep.

Stride didn't want to put into words the thoughts that were stringing like watery beads into place – click, click, click – the late phone call, his mother's vacant stare, his absent father . . . click, click . . . click.

'They don't know yet.' Her voice was almost inaudible.

'Don't know what?' His voice was high-pitched and unsteady.

'Frank.'

'Dad? What? What's happened?'

She took a breath. 'It was the coastguard – no – the police, ringing from the coastguard's. There was a mayday call . . .'

Stride sat, his hands between his knees, his body trembling. Annie, his older sister, appeared in the doorway. Annie glanced from her mother to Stride to the phone, her mouth open expectantly. Then she sat on the floor in front of the fire, without taking her eyes off the phone, and Stride knew she'd heard everything he had heard.

They sat huddled by the dying fire as the storm raged outside. With morning, the wind dropped and the phone stayed silent. Annie rested her head on Stride's shoulder as they stared into the coals. When the knock came, Stride's mother rose and walked to the door as if through water, and Annie tightened her arm around Stride's waist.

Stride heard low voices in the hall, and saw his mum, dark against the hall light, with Gramps. He held her. She was pale and staggered as they came into the room, and Gramps had tears on his cheeks.

'I'm not wearing a suit,' Stride said in a low voice to his mother who was at the table drinking black coffee.

'Dignam, I've hired a suit and you'll wear it. It's . . . respectful.'

Stride cringed. Dignam was his real name. It was Grandpa Smithson's name and his father's, and *his* father's, now passed down to Stride. And when his mother called him 'Dignam' it was always a bad sign.

Stride's voice rose. 'Dad wouldn't care what I wore. He didn't care about clothes . . .' his voice broke as he remembered his father's navy fisherman's jumper with frayed sleeves and a neck that had grown loose over the years, his discoloured jeans torn at the knees and rubber boots folded over from the top.

'*He* knows he's got my respect. I don't care if anyone

else knows or not.' His voice dropped. 'It doesn't matter what I wear, it won't change anything!' He clenched his teeth to stop the welling tears. 'And anyway,' he slowed, breathed deeply and steadied himself, 'if I wear a suit, I can't take Ferd.'

His mother stopped, the cup midway to her mouth and stared at Stride.

'Ferd? Dignam, you will not take that cockatoo to your father's funeral.'

The big white bird turned at the sound of his name. He ruffled his feathers and clicked his beak as he balanced on the bar stool by the door. The wrinkled pouches of skin around his black eyes folded and refolded as he looked from one to the other.

'Ferd was Dad's mate.' Stride stood, and held tightly to the back of a kitchen chair. His knuckles whitened as he clenched and unclenched his hands. 'I thought this funeral was supposed to be about Dad.' Tears spilled down his cheeks.

'Stride . . .' Annie was sitting on the floor, home-work spread around her. 'Leave it!' Annie's voice was sharp and her eyes shone with unshed tears. The battle between Stride and his mother became a silent one. They stared at each other, their blue eyes locked, neither prepared to give in.

The fire popped, showering sparks onto the hearth rug where they glowed red for a moment and then blinked out.

Stride looked away. 'Ferd's got to be there – they were friends . . . since Dad was a kid.'

His mother was silent. She stared into her coffee. Annie doodled on the knee of her jeans with her pen, her legs drawn up under her chin. Her dark curly hair was untidy and the way it hung over her forehead reminded Stride of his dad. She was Stride's sister, but shared little in looks, interests or personality. They were born on either side of midnight, twelve months apart, Annie, late on the last day of September, Stride early on the first of October.

She glanced up at him and her eyes softened. Stride's shoulders dropped and he wiped his face on his sleeve. He stretched his fingers out to the big white cockatoo. The bird watched him without moving.

'Come on,' Stride whispered. He stroked Ferd's scaly claws, but Ferd edged away, eyeing his fingers suspiciously. His seed bowl sat on the stool untouched. He had hardly eaten for days. Stride made a clicking sound. The cockatoo blinked, tamped his beak with his cylindrical grey tongue and made a jangling sound. Stride scratched behind his yellow crest. Ferd tilted his head forwards and shut his upside down eyelids, half lifting his left claw to help scratch. Stride offered his arm again, but Ferd shuffled away from him, refusing to step onto his wrist. Stride rubbed one weary arm over his face, sighed, and walked heavily out the door without looking back.

Outside it was dark – a soft drizzling darkness that muffled the roar of the sea and blurred the single street light on the main road. He pulled the hood of his windcheater forward, pressed his hands into his pockets and headed towards the pale smudge of path leading to the beach.

At the beginning of the path, he hesitated, turned, ran back and pushed open the door of the darkened hallway. He felt along the wall for the row of pegs behind the door. His fingers slid along the timber boards, patting in the gloom until he felt the thick rough texture of his father's Bluey. His hands ran over the collar, the sleeves and down into the pockets. For a moment he leaned his head against the coarse wool and breathed in – a faint smell of salty air, physical labour and fish, and his chest filled with longing.

Nestled in the crease of the pocket, just where his father left it, Stride found what he was searching for: Ferd's chain and the leather band his father wore on his

wrist when he carried him. Stride's fingers closed
slowly around it. The chain clinked and Stride held his
breath; he didn't want his mum or Annie to hear. He
listened to the hiss of the open fire and their subdued
voices, and carefully lifted the chain and band from his
father's coat and left the house.

Down on the beach, beyond the tree line, he could
make out the shifting dance of breaking surf. He
stopped just below the dunes, squatted and carefully
slid the leather band onto his wrist. The buckle
wanted to settle into the familiar groove that fitted his
father's muscular wrist. He tightened it, one, then two
more notches, poked the metal spike through the
hole and pushed the strap under the steel clasp.
There was something comforting about the smooth
leather, blackened and worn from the years of contact
with his father's skin. He fastened the chain to the
band, ran his hands along it to the other end and felt
for the clip that attached to the ring Ferd wore on
his leg.

'One of these days we'll be mates, Ferd . . . and you
won't miss him anymore . . .' His whisper faltered. He
twisted the clip over and over in his other hand, rose,
and walked along the beach, leaning into the wind and
rain . . .

Stride woke to onshore gusts that sent the rain hurtling against his window. The sea beyond the ti-tree was grey and formless. He swung out of bed and gazed down at his unwashed feet – grains of sand still edged his toes from where he'd run barefoot along the beach last night. He felt the band on his wrist and stroked the soft hide. He lifted it and sniffed – leather and flesh – and ran his lips across it, over and over . . .

The suit his mother had hired for him for the funeral hung on the back of his door. He stood and roughly lifted the plastic cover. The movement dislodged the jacket and it slid to the floor where Stride left it.

Out in the kitchen, Ferd was perched in the same spot he had been yesterday, and the three days before that, his food bowl still undisturbed.

'Hello boy.' The bird blinked and changed feet. Stride held up the chain and rested his wrist on the bench in front of him. Ferd squawked quietly and glanced down, but resumed his passive stance, his eyes staring into the distance.

Stride sighed, took a handful of birdseed and held it up to him. Ferd showed no interest. Stride scratched his crest and Ferd tilted his head, making his soft jangly sound, but that was all. Stride placed his wrist closer where Ferd could step onto it, but Ferd just blinked.

Stride gently rubbed his nose along Ferd's beak. He knew then that he wouldn't take Ferd on his arm to the funeral. Ferd wanted to stay just where he was . . . Stride could wear the suit, and his mum would be happy . . .

2 Funeral

Within an hour, stomach rumbling, but not with hunger, Stride was seated in the hearse with his mother and sister. Annie was staring out the window. The short black coat she wore made her skin seem paler than usual, and her dark hair was pinned back from her face. Stride reached out and touched her hand. Her face softened and he saw the dimple in her cheek deepen for a moment.

'Pity Ferd couldn't come.'

'Wasn't meant to be I guess . . . You okay?'

Annie nodded.

'No blubbing in public, you hear?'

Annie smiled. 'I'll blub, nothing surer. You?'

Stride sighed and nodded. 'Yep.'

Their mother turned briefly towards them, her eyes hidden behind dark glasses, her fingers tucked into her palms.

Outside, the waves beyond the foreshore churned and ran at odd angles to the beach. Stride wondered if the storm would resurrect his father's boat — somehow lift it from the sea bed and send it bubbling, spouting water, back to the shore. He imagined the deck awash with silver, gaping fish. He imagined his dad's unshaven face, laughing beneath his dark curly hair as he bent over the watery deck . . .

'Remember Easter?' Stride murmured. 'Remember the ray?'

'Yeah.'

'The biggest one dad had ever seen.'

'Dad made calamari.'

'We fought about which bunk we were going to sleep in.'

'I won.'

'Yeah, you won.'

Annie's hands twisted in her lap. Then her chin trembled and she looked away.

After the funeral, there was a wake at the Point Wondai Co-operative. Stride's dad had helped establish the co-op years ago as a way of surviving when big business threatened to send them all under with their huge, well-equipped trawlers and aggressive marketing. The co-op had saved most of the local fishermen from bankruptcy.

'Anything for Frank,' one of the fishermen had told Stride's mum. 'We want a send-off that's worthy of him.'

And they had. It seemed that everyone from Seal Bay and Point Wondai had turned up. Trestle tables were loaded with platters of fresh seafood and rich homemade cakes. Everyone had a story to tell about Frank – the seasoned fisherman, the man who carried a cockatoo wherever he went, the proud father who took his kids on his boat with him more than any other fisherman.

Stride appreciated all the hearty words spoken about his dad and the number of people who had slapped his back, shaken his hand, given him a hug, and murmured, 'Sorry.' But now he wanted to be back at Seal Bay, wearing his own clothes, in his own house where the walls still carried a faint scent of his dad.

Annie was with a group of friends, sitting with her closest friend, Soula. The others were talking and laughing, but Annie just sat, her arm across Soula's shoulders. Stride tried to catch her eye, but she didn't look up.

He knelt beside her. 'I'm going home.'

She hesitated. 'How?'

'I'll start walking. I'll get a lift I reckon.'

'Mum doesn't like you hitching.'

'I'm not hitching; but if someone I know stops, I'll take it.'

'Where's Mum? Do you know how long she's staying?'

'Dunno.'

Her eyes darted around the room.

Soula spoke. 'We'll give you a lift, Annie. Your mum'll be here for ages.'

'Okay.' She turned to Stride. 'Be careful. Don't do anything dumb, will you?'

Stride shook his head. 'Are you sure you want to stay?'

She pressed her lips together and nodded. 'Yeah . . . I'm okay.'

He rose and left quickly through a side door.

The heavy clouds that had brought rain all week had retreated south and Stride loped down the main street, shiny with puddles that reflected the yellowing evening sky.

Ten minutes later, a Landrover pulled up. It was Dooks's mum. Dooks was Stride's mate from school; they'd been buddies since kinder.

'Can I give you a lift, Stride?' she asked. 'You'll have to hop in the back; I'm loaded up in the front.'

Stride opened the back door and sat on the straw, chaff dust and dog hair. He pulled off the suit jacket and threw it down on the bench seat beside him. Dooks's mum chattered about how the rain was a blessing and a curse – once the hot weather hit, there'd be so much long grass, it would make for a bad bushfire summer. She didn't expect responses and Stride gave none. Both of them were comfortable that way. After her conversation had run its course, she whistled a low, melancholy tune that seemed to start nowhere and finish in the same place.

She dropped Stride off at the start of her own driveway, about half a kilometre from his house, and Stride jogged the rest of the way, the suit jacket slipping back and forth on his arm as he ran.

In the kitchen, Ferd was still perched on the bench.

'Hello, old fella. Your beak's wet – good boy, you've been drinking.'

Ferd blinked. Stride checked his seed bowl and thought there was a small dent in the middle. He flicked around for husks, but found none. What if Ferd starved himself to death? The muscles between Stride's shoulder blades cramped.

He swung his arms as he went to his room, where he pulled off the suit pants and his good shirt and slipped on jeans and a T-shirt. He smoothed the bird band on his wrist, and collected the chain from where he'd left it on his desk and clicked it onto the band. And suddenly he knew.

He struggled, urgently pulling his T-shirt over his head, tangling the chain. Starting again, he threaded the chain through an arm hole until the chain was coiled in his hand.

He raced through the living room and down the hall. His hands moved swiftly across the wall behind the door as they had the previous evening, until he found the pegs jutting from the wall. He stopped, his heart thumping, his palms prickling. He groped for the light switch. The dim globe flicked on – the pegs were bare.

He felt like all the air had been knocked out of his lungs. He ran to Annie's room. It was spotless as usual – nothing out of place, no clothes on the floor or the bed, all hung carefully in the wardrobe. In his mum's room he flung open the double wardrobe. Her side was full, shelves stacked with neatly folded jumpers, shoes in rows, shirts, pants and dresses hung spaciously. He opened his father's side.

'NO!' His voice reverberated in the empty cupboard. He slammed the door, shock pounding against his temples.

He ran to the pantry. Opening it, he found the torch that hung there. Back outside, twilight had turned to night, a silky blackness he could almost feel on his skin.

He flashed the light around the garage in swift jerking arcs and almost missed it: a trunk in the back corner. He lifted the lid: his dad's felt hat, his other fishing jumper, his holey jeans, his old Bluey, his cap, the one with the greasy rim. He dropped the torch. The light buckled and was gone. He scrabbled frantically for it, his hand closing around the hard plastic. He whacked it with his hand and the light flickered back on. It slipped through his fingers again, into the box where he fumbled beneath his father's clothes, as wafts of Frank floated up to him, and tears blurred his eyesight.

Stride held his dad's singlet to his face and wiped his eyes, blew his nose and let his cheek rest on the navy cotton. He grabbed the torch and gathered some of his dad's clothes, wrapped them into a bundle, and stumbled through the darkness back to the house.

In his bedroom, he pushed aside a pile of his shoes on the floor of his wardrobe and one by one folded his father's clothes and lay them in the space he'd made, smoothing them as he lay each one down – the Lee Jeans, the woollen shirts, the mittens. He placed the Bluey and the cap on his bed, along with the boots and the chain.

He ran his fingers over the upturned collar of the Bluey and the boots. He slipped one arm into the Bluey, then the other. It was too big, but it felt good. He flipped the cap on. The boots were uncomfortable, moulded long ago into a shape that Stride would never quite suit.

He studied himself in the mirror. Strands of blond hair escaped from the cap. He tucked them up inside and patted the cap down around his forehead the way his dad used to. He flicked the upturned collar of the coat as Frank did against the wind, hunched his shoulders and hurried into the kitchen.

Stride stared at Ferd without speaking. He was

hardly breathing, feeling the prickle of the Bluey against his skin, the smooth band of the cap across his forehead. They gazed at each other. Ferd stared straight at Stride unblinking. Then his eyelids closed for an instant, and he lifted his crest, slowly at first, letting it drop down into the smooth 'j' it made on his neck. Stride didn't move. Ferd threw his crest forward. He screeched, flapped his wings and, with his eyes on Stride, side-stepped along the bench towards him, bobbing his head up and down, holding his wings out from his body. He stopped, lifted one claw, and held it in midair. Stride did what he'd seen his father do countless times: he ran the fingers of one hand between Ferd's wings and with the other, smoothed the feathers on his chest. Ferd's hovering foot came down onto Stride's wrist and with slow measured movements, he stepped up Stride's arm, his eyes unblinking. Then he leaned across, grabbed the collar of the coat and swung himself up, his claws clinging to the fabric. Once on Stride's shoulder, he threw his crest up and jangled loudly as if he was laughing.

Stride lifted the food bowl. Ferd bent his head to a sunflower seed and, his eyes on Stride, turned it around his tongue. Finally he began cracking and scraping it with his lower beak. Stride breathed out.

Stride heard Annie push open the front door and the hollow sound of her footsteps on the floorboards in the unlit hall. She stopped, and Stride heard her suck in her breath. And then she screamed.

Stride swung around. Ferd screeched and lifted his wings, his crest upright, a seed held in his upright claw, halfway to his beak.

Annie's hand clung to the door frame and her jacket slid silently to the floor. Her breath came in shuddering gasps and her mouth moved, but without sound. Then, a sob.

'Annie?'

'Stride? What . . . what do you . . . what are you doing?' She shook her head, tears spilling down her cheeks, her nose running unchecked. 'I thought . . . I thought . . . you were . . .' But she couldn't say it, and then it came in a rush. 'Oh Stride, I thought you were dad.'

Stride swallowed and coughed nervously.

'I wasn't expecting anyone home so soon.' He paused, then patted the couch beside him with his free hand. 'Hey, come here . . . Look, Ferd's eating. He made the mistake you did, 'cept it's . . . ah . . . not scary for him.'

Annie sniffed, and tried to smile. She sat next to Stride and Ferd bobbed his head up and down and lifted the seed in his claw to his beak. He cracked the husk, then stretched for another seed that Stride had put between his lips. Ferd took it triumphantly in his beak and threw back his head lifting his crest, raising a claw while he screeched raucously.

Stride laughed aloud at his success. Annie smiled, her hands tightly between her knees. Stride brushed her cheek with the back of his hand.

'Sorry – that must have been . . . freaky . . .'

Annie nodded, wiping her nose between her thumb and forefinger, colour creeping back into her cheeks and lips. She leaned against the couch and stroked Ferd, her face against Frank's rough coat. She smoothed down Ferd's crest, letting her fingers ride gently over his feathers.

3 Trio

In the morning, Stride woke to the sound of Ferd screeching. Early silver light drifted through the window. Stride propped himself on one elbow. He could see by the droppings on the old towel on the floor that Ferd had perched in one spot the whole night – on the back of the chair. His crest was up and his head was tilted to one side.

Stride smiled. 'What is it, you crazy bird?'

Ferd bobbed his head up and down, stretched one wing and a leg, and squawked again.

'Pipe down, will ya – you'll wake everyone.'

Ferd crouched and launched, landing on the window ledge. He tapped his beak on the glass.

'No way – you're not going out yet.'

Stride swung himself out of bed. He dragged on jeans and a T-shirt. His father's coat and cap hung where he'd left them, dark shadows on the back of the door.

Ferd watched him from the window ledge. He blinked at Stride.

'Okay, okay,' Stride muttered. He scooped up the coat and shrugged into it. Ferd launched himself again, landing on Stride's shoulder. He nibbled the peak of the cap as Stride pulled it on, his black eye fixed on Stride.

'You're a mad bird . . .' Stride murmured. He stroked Ferd's throat, ruffling the feathers, enjoying the chalkiness in the skin beneath. Ferd tamped his tongue back and forth against the inside of his beak and made his soft, slow jangly sound. He half shut his eyes, his lids wrinkled and elastic.

'Hungry?'

Ferd bobbed his head up and down and flapped his wings.

'Careful, Ferd!' Stride edged Ferd's wings into place and settled him low on his shoulder.

Annie was curled on the couch in her doona, early morning music videos playing softly on the television.

'What are you doing up so early?'

'Couldn't sleep. What about you?'

'Fine. But Ferd woke me early wanting to get out.'

'Yeah, I'd just gone off to sleep finally when I heard him kicking up a racket.'

'Sorry. He was banging on the glass.'

'Did you let him out?'

'No . . . not comfortable doing that. Give me a few weeks before I take risks with him.'

'He's pretty comfy with you now.'

'Yeah, cos he thinks I'm dad. Wonder what he'll do when he finds out the truth.'

'I don't think he'll go anywhere.'

Stride lifted the pan off the hook and began breaking eggs into a bowl. 'Want eggs?'

'No thanks . . . not hungry.'

'Maybe I'll do some for Mum.'

'Mum doesn't eat before three coffees . . . I wouldn't waste my time. Just put the jug on.'

Stride poured the beaten eggs into the pan. He pressed the toaster down and flicked the switch on the electric jug. Ferd launched, gliding to roost on the kitchen door just as Mum scuffed down the hallway in her dressing gown and slippers. She sank onto the couch beside Annie, yawned, pulled her long hair into a knot with one hand and rested the other on Annie's shoulder.

'Coffee, Mum?'

She turned to Stride and her hand stopped twisting her hair.

'Stride! What are . . .?'

'What?' Stride asked, and waved the eggslice.

Mum groaned and shut her eyes. 'Do I have to spell it out?'

'What?' Stride's voice was irritated.

'God, Stride – you're wearing your father's clothes. It's . . . it's unsettling to say the least.'

'Oh.' He looked down at the coat and back at his mother. 'Sorry. It's the only way for Ferd to feel normal. He's comfortable with me dressed like this. That's a *good* thing.'

His mother sighed. Ferd clung to the top of the door watching with black eyes. 'Well, it might be fine for Ferd, but it's very uncomfortable for the rest of us.' She appealed to Annie, but Annie concentrated on pulling the doona up to her chin and patting it flat where it puffed up over her knees.

'Okay, okay . . . but I thought you'd be happy – Ferd's eating again.' Stride slipped the coat and cap off, throwing them over the back of the bar stool.

Ferd mumbled from his perch then flew down to the bench, landed by the fruit basket, nibbled an apple and dropped the skin onto the bench, all the time emitting small 'crrks' of contentment.

Stride made no further offers of coffee, slammed the cupboard when he took out his plate, and skidded his fork across to the breakfast bar. He sat with his back to his mother and Annie as he ate.

When he finished his eggs he turned back to see them sitting end to end on the couch, his mum's feet tucked under the doona.

Stride left the dirty dishes on the bench and stalked off to his room, jamming the coat and cap under his arm. Ferd flew into Stride's bedroom, the apple core clutched in his beak, and Stride kicked the door shut.

Ferd was soon flying around the house just like old times. Stride still wore his dad's coat and cap. Sometimes his mum coughed and left the room, and once she snapped, 'It isn't right, Stride!' Stride avoided her eyes and kept on wearing his father's clothes.

Annie occasionally leaned in to him and rested her hand on the coat sleeve. Sometimes she would press her nose against the coarse weave, breathing in, her eyes closed. He said nothing, but as her eyes opened, he smiled at her and she smiled back and both felt a lightness that lasted for the rest of the day.

Stride set up Ferd's night perch outside his bedroom window with a long lightweight rope tied to the perch and clipped onto the ring on Ferd's leg. Ferd was content to roost there. Stride saw him last thing in the evening and brought him inside first thing in the morning.

Soon Stride and Ferd were taking walks together down to the beach or into Seal Bay, Ferd perched on Stride's wrist or shoulder.

Soula's dad, Dominic, called to him on the street as he parked his ute. 'Hey, Stride, how's your cockatoo going?'

'He's good.'

'That arm of yours getting stronger, eh?' Dominic smiled, his teeth white against his weather-beaten face.

Stride peeled back the leather on his wrist, proudly showing the pale untanned strip on his arm. 'And my arm doesn't ache anymore.'

Dominic eyed Stride's biceps and nodded. 'Just like your old man, eh?'

Stride grinned, shrugged and ran his hand down Ferd's back, just like Frank used to.

Outside of school, Stride took Ferd wherever he went. Ferd ate the quarters of apple Stride rested on the back of his arm, peeling them with his lower beak as he watched Stride with dark eyes, the two of them sitting against the north side of the house where the late winter sun warmed the flaking white wall.

It was an afternoon near the end of term and Annie was practising her flute inside. She stopped and Stride heard raised voices. There was silence, a door slammed and Annie appeared from the side of the house, her flute in her hand.

'Shove over. I need that bit of sun.'

'It's my bit of sun, but here . . .' and Stride smoothed the spot next to him.

Stride dropped a handful of seed into the top pocket of his shirt. Ferd, perched on his shoulder, dipped headfirst into the pocket, and overbalanced. He righted himself by gripping Stride's shirt with his claws and beak, leaving red welts down Stride's chest, making consoling 'crrk' sounds.

'Watch those claws, Ferd.'

Ferd repeated the action, this time clinging to the front of Stride's shirt bringing out seeds each time and chirping small congratulatory 'crrks' as he looked Stride directly in the eye.

Stride nodded. 'Yes, you're the smartest bird I know.' Ferd straightened, climbed back onto Stride's shoulder and nibbled at Stride's ear lobe. Stride tickled Ferd's rough grey toes, while Ferd crooned in his corrugated voice. Annie's eyes softened, her cheeks dimpled and she smiled.

'You and Mum fighting?' Stride asked.

Annie sighed. 'Yes . . . again. It's always over stupid little things – emptying the dishwasher, folding the clothes in a certain way – you know how it is. We never used to fight. She's so tight.'

'Tell me about it. She's hardly spoken to me since I resurrected Dad's clothes.'

'I spoke to Gramps about it last night. He said we should be sympathetic. He said to remember she's grieving.'

'I guess, but we are too . . .' He paused. 'Anyway, she's the grown up, she should be holding it all together, right?'

'I wish.'

'At least I can talk to Ferd . . . We never fight. He never loses it if I don't tidy my room or clear the table.' They grinned.

29

'It'll get better.' Her fingers followed the curve of Ferd's wing. 'I have to practise some more. My exam's next week.'

'Good.' Stride smiled. 'Feels like . . . before . . . you know . . . old times.' She nodded, and soon the breathy, metallic voice of the flute drifted again through the open window above his head.

Five minutes later Stride's mum emerged with her gardening gloves and pulled the weeds that flourished on the damp southern side of the garage.

'I really need some input to maintain this place,' she called to Stride. 'The lawn needs a trim. The mower needs some fuel so can you walk to the petrol station and get a can of . . . what is it? Four-stroke or two-stroke? I can never remember.'

'It would be easier if we drove in the car.'

'Fuel always spills in the car and the smell never goes away.'

'She's finished with Annie and now it's our turn, Ferd,' he murmured getting to his feet.

'What was that?' His mother turned, a bundle of weeds in her arms.

'Nothing.'

'I'd like it done before next weekend.'

'Why?'

'If you do it before it gets too long, there's less raking, it's a bit easier.'

'A few days won't make much difference.'

'Stride, don't push me. I've asked and I want it done.' She bent to pick up a fallen thistle.

'Now that Dad's not here for you to nag.'

Stride's mother swung around, her voice quiet. 'How dare you!'

Stride didn't speak, but turned and made for the beach without looking back, Ferd's screeching voice receding across the sand.

Spring came and the sun grew warmer. The days lengthened and Annie planted basil seedlings by the brick chimney. The lawn thickened and a pair of swallows built a mud nest under the eaves.

And finally the day came when Stride put his dad's Bluey and cap, folded and smoothed, back into the dark corner of his wardrobe.

4 New Year

It was summer, and school holidays. Stride stretched and kicked off the cotton sheet.

'Come on, boy.' He unclipped Ferd's chained leg and brought him in through the open window. The sky was pearly and the sound of the surf beckoned like a favourite song.

It was almost four months since Ferd had first squawked with pleasure, accompanying Stride as he jogged into the cold wind on the beach all the way to the lagoon at the north end of the bay. It was just over three months since Ferd's first ride on Stride's bike, when they cycled from Seal Bay to Point Wondai to buy birdseed from the pet shop. Ferd had craned his neck forward and spread his wings, his claws clamped to the handlebars. He learned quickly to anticipate the rough spots on the road, to crouch and brace himself as they went over the bumps. He screeched and threw his crest forward. Passers-by pointed and nudged their children, 'Look at the cocky!' Stride pretended not to notice and stared straight ahead, but whispered under his breath, 'Stop showing off, Ferd.' Ferd bobbed up and down and threw his head back with a wide jangling sound that Stride was sure was laughter.

And it was two weeks since Annie had bought Stride a new leather wristband to replace the one that had fallen apart, on that first hollow fatherless Christmas eve.

Now it almost felt as if Ferd had always been his and Stride found it hard to remember how it was without the cockatoo as a constant companion. He stroked Ferd's back with both hands, gently drawing out his wings and then tucking them back. Ferd jostled his feathers into place and bobbed his head up and down, muttering sounds that were almost human, but indecipherable.

Frank had never taught Ferd how to talk. 'They've got their own language. They don't need ours,' he'd said to Stride. 'He's not a performer, he's just himself,' he'd added as Ferd nibbled at a stray thread on the cuff of his jumper. It wasn't the first jumper he'd joyfully unravelled, pulling the wool until half a sleeve was just a tangle of wool on the floor. 'Bad boy,' Frank had murmured mildly, stroking him.

Although it was summer, the day was cool and overcast. Around the headland the sea mist hung as if resting. Stride squinted at the horizon – the sea and sky blending blue-grey.

'Dignam, have you got that bird in there? It's not healthy having a bird indoors,' she called from the other side of the door. 'He'd be much happier outside.'

'Mum, he loves being inside. Dad always said he needed people.'

'Dignam, I'm not going to argue about it.'

He shouldn't have mentioned Dad.

Ferd flew to the top of the wardrobe to pick the putty out of the filled crack in the plaster. Stride waved his arms at him, but Ferd seemed to know Stride couldn't yell at him while his mother was listening – the crack in the wall grew bigger and flakes of plaster fell to the floor.

'Dignam!'

'What?'

'You've got him in there haven't you.'

Stride quickly kicked the pile of plaster under the bed. He wondered whether he should risk shoving Ferd in the wardrobe. Last time Ferd had picked the buttons off his only dress shirt, the one he'd worn to the funeral. Secretly, Stride thought Ferd had been pretty smart to manage that in the dark, but it hadn't amused his mother.

He slid out of his room, quickly closing the door behind him. His mother glared at him. She was dressed for work in a strappy sundress and sandals, her fair hair swept up and secured with a comb.

'Stride, I know your father loved that bird, but it's time he was outside. He's very destructive. You know that. I don't want the house damaged. Your father . . .' she stopped. 'There's no one to fix window frames and re-plaster holes, and I can't afford to pay anyone to do it.'

'Dad never got around to those jobs anyway. You never worried before. Why now?'

She fiddled with a nail.

'Just do as I ask without an argument for once.'

He heard a clunk and guessed Ferd was slowly tearing his room apart.

'Well, I'll see . . .' he mumbled and slid back through his door, slamming it shut. Ferd bobbed his head up and down and lifted his wings. A strip of timber beading from around the wardrobe door lay splintered on the floor.

Stride groaned. 'Let's get out of here!'

He took Ferd's chain from behind the door. Ferd screeched and flew down onto Stride's shoulder and tweaked his ear.

'Stand still, Ferd.'

As Stride clipped the chain onto Ferd's leg, Ferd dived for Stride's hand as he often did when he chained him, and gashed his knuckle. Stride swore under his breath, wiping the blood on his shorts. Ferd raised his crest, beak wide, and screeched his jangling laughter. Stride clipped the chain to his wrist, took a handful of birdseed and wedged the door closed before climbing out the window. Ferd, on his arm, squawked and flapped, grabbing for Stride's hair to balance himself. Stride landed on the spongy buffalo grass that crept up the walls outside his room. He steadied Ferd and pulled his window shut, staring for a minute at the house.

It was an old, square, bare-faced place, set in the middle of a knoll, surrounded by pungent buffalo grass that ran down the hill on all sides, like custard over pudding, disappearing into the shade of the ti-trees on the slope. On a clear day, the whole coastline was visible, from Point Wondai to the north, around the bay to the next headland Harper's Lookout in the south.

Directly below the line of scrub was the small foreshore camping ground. During the summer holidays it was always full. Campers came back year after year, sliding tent pegs into the same holes. They were drawn by the curve of Seal Bay, the haunting call of the tawny frogmouth owls, and the ringtail possums that whistled in thin voices to one another at lamp-lighting time each dusk.

From Stride's house, there was a tunnel through the ti-trees that ended at the edge of the camping ground, where it became a sandy track that led down to the beach.

Stride followed it now to where a big orange tent had been pitched by the track since yesterday. A group of kids rushed out as Stride approached.

'Can we pat him?'

'Can I have a hold?'

'Can I mind him for you?'

'Hello, Cocky! Hello. Hello. Hello.'

'Why doesn't he talk?'

'He's not a performer,' Stride muttered. 'Watch out, he might bite, he's not used to crowds.'

Ferd lifted his wings, screeched and threw his

crest forward. The kids squealed and Ferd flapped wildly. Stride tried to calm him, tripped on a tent peg and landed face down on the ground, spitting crumbs of dirt and sand. His left arm was wrenched up as Ferd rose into the air to save himself, and the kids scattered.

'Careful!'

The sharp voice made Stride look up quickly. A girl with a face full of freckles, glared down at him. 'I hope you didn't injure her.'

Stride stared at the girl and frowned. 'Keep your pants on.' He struggled to his feet fighting to maintain some dignity. 'It's not as if I meant to fall over . . .'

She ignored him and turned to Ferd who had re-settled on Stride's shoulder. Ferd lifted his wings, squawked and danced his crest up and down. The girl burst out laughing.

'You great big show-off. Here, are you hungry girl?' From her pocket she pulled out a handful of sunflower kernels. Ferd leaned forward and, watching the girl's face all the time, took a seed in his beak, deftly twirling it on his dry tongue.

Stride pulled his arm away so fast, Ferd over-balanced and screeched in surprise.

'Ferd's a boy . . . and he's not allowed to have too many sunflower seeds,' Stride muttered. 'They make cockatoos sick.'

The girl stared at Stride with clear blue eyes and smiled. 'Oh, okay then.' She said it lightly, dropping the seed back into the pocket of her jeans. 'I'll save the seed for the parrots.'

'They make parrots sick, too,' Stride growled. Her smile suggested she thought she knew a little more than he did on the topic. Her bare toe tapped the sand and she folded her arms over her T-shirt. She was about the same age as Stride and had hair the colour of the dark red chooks Gramps kept. It was matted into dread-locks and tied back from her face.

She smiled again. 'Like my dreads?'

Stride hesitated, unsure of what to say.

A laugh burbled from the base of her throat. 'Cool huh?'

Stride rubbed his grazed knee and checked Ferd's chain.

'Uh . . . yeah . . . whatever . . .' he mumbled, not looking at her.

He turned abruptly, taking care that Ferd was stable, and made for the beach. Ferd lifted his great wings and flapped, watching the girl and nodding his head up and down to her. Stride thought he heard the girl's burbling laugh again, and broke angrily intro a trot.

There had been a high tide and the beach was free of footprints. The morning sun was strengthening and Stride jogged north along the sand. Ferd lifted his wings and leaned forward, squawking in delight.

Normally Stride would encourage Ferd with a 'Go, boy!', but the girl had irritated him, like a stone in his sock, and he was silent until the lagoon.

They reached the dunes that rose behind the beach, high and curved, dimpled into a thousand ridges by sea breezes. Clumps of bone-white grass, leaning inland, dotted the banks. Stride slowed and was panting by the time he reached the crest of the dunes. He knelt, facing the steep drop to the lagoon on the other side. The lagoon was deep and clear, tinged yellow with ti-tree tannin. Schools of small speckled fish darted in unison, left, right, left right.

Behind him was the constant sh . . . sh . . . sh . . . of the surf, while by the lagoon there was an almost eerie hush. The misty silence was broken by a pair of plovers calling, sharp and mournful.

Few people came here. Access was difficult with thick coastal scrub to the west of the lagoon and this side, the sand dunes, tall and daunting.

A sudden movement to Stride's left caught his attention. He scanned the dunes and thought he saw a flash of something, but then it was gone. Ferd, too, was alert and watchful, unsettled into silence, his normal chatter absent.

'You're imagining things,' Stride murmured, stroking Ferd's back, but he kept a look-out all the same.

Gradually the mist lifted, the sky showed blue and the sun grew warmer. Stride and Ferd spent the rest of the morning uninterrupted, wading in the lagoon, watching fish and listening to the shimmering insect hum that rose from the other side of the lagoon.

5 Beginner's Luck

The next day felt like true summer. Heat rose from the buffalo grass bringing a sweet earthy smell into the house. The sea was turquoise, the waves glaringly bright and the black rocks at Point Wondai glistened.

Stride opened the window and brought Ferd in off his perch.

'Have to clean up today,' he told Ferd. 'Mum's all, "No pocket money till the house is spotless!"' He kicked two mismatched shoes under the bed and flung dirty socks into a pile by the door. 'Well, that's the bedroom tidied. Let's go do your space.'

He clipped Ferd to his wrist, slipped on old runners, and paused briefly to run his hand down the curved edge of the surfboard that leaned against the wall, feeling for any undetected dings in the fibreglass.

'Waves sound good today, Ferd. Let's get this job out of the way and hit the beach.' He hesitated. Ferd stretched forward, his eyes quizzical, and made a gentle 'ccrk'. Stride stroked his head and Ferd tamped his beak with his tongue.

In the shed, Stride grabbed the spade, wheelbarrow, bucket and scrubbing brush. Under the perch he scooped up the birdseed, husks and droppings and shovelled them into the wheelbarrow. Ferd balanced on the handles of the wheelbarrow, his chain attached to the barrow's metal shaft. He watched Stride's every move with interest, his head on one side, intermittently carking at him.

When the ground was cleared, Stride filled the bucket with soapy water and scrubbed the weatherboards and the perch until his arm ached and the grain of the timber was visible.

'Good enough to get my pocket money this week I reckon, Ferd. I'll have enough to get my own board soon, eh?' Ferd blinked and scratched his head with his right foot, while Stride emptied the wheelbarrow into the compost and dumped everything else back in the shed.

'Let's eat.' Ferd bobbed his head and Stride tickled behind his almost invisible ears. Ferd closed his eyes and clicked his blunt tongue against his slightly open beak.

Inside, Stride spread left-over pasta sauce on bread, sprinkled it with cheese and pushed it under the grill. He was squatting to watch the cheese melt and bubble when the phone rang.

'Eh, Dooksie . . . Yeah, course . . . Sure. Well, it is your board. Good waves? About eleven . . . Yeah, if that's cool with you . . . Yeah, well, I was just telling Ferd I'll be able to get my own soon. Cruso said he'd give me a good deal. I've asked him to look out for a second-hand one, but it'll still be about three hundred I reckon . . . Yeah? Okay, see you then.'

Stride hung up the phone and pushed back on his seat, teetering on the back legs of the bar stool. He thumped the bench with his fist; he wasn't ready to give the board back yet. He swung the stool upright, turned the griller to its lowest setting and hurried to his room. He carefully layed the surfboard on his bed, ran his eye over it, gave it a quick wipe with a towel then carried it out to the living room.

While he ate his toasted sandwich, he watched the line of surf through the window. He had always watched waves, as far back as he could remember. He understood them – their size, shape, and strength, how they were affected by tides and storms and how they rolled in sets, the impact of offshore and onshore winds. It was inevitable that he'd take up surfing.

He used to wish his dad had been an old surfer – like Dooks's dad who had a surfer's squint and the leathery hide to prove he'd been out there, winter and summer. His own dad's understanding of the sea had been a fisherman's. Stride had been proud of what his dad knew, no question, but he would have liked to discuss sets and barrels and the thrill of the feel of the wall of water on his hand as he shot through a tube.

He slid his plate into the sink and swept the crumbs off the bench onto the floor.

'Ferd?' The bird swooped down from the top of the pantry and at the last minute, tilted his wings and swung up to roost on the living room door. Stride could nearly always predict where he would land, even when he wasn't watching him. When he heard the beat of wings and felt the movement of air they made, he imagined Ferd outside among huge eucalyptus trees, winging to the topmost branches, screeching, or hanging from boughs picking seeds and nuts with his powerful beak, letting husks ricochet to the forest floor.

'Come on you, we're outta here. I hope you haven't pooped inside – Mum will kill me.'

Both he and Ferd bobbed low as they hurried through the ti-tree tunnel, Dooks's surfboard under Stride's arm.

Now there were two sites to avoid – the orange tent with all the kids, and the dreadlock girl, except he had no idea where she was camping. He didn't know if she was camping at all, but he knew she wasn't local so he just assumed she was one of the city tourists who blew in each summer and thought they owned the beach.

Dooks was standing at the high tide mark two hundred metres up the beach. Stride knew it was Dooks from the odd angle of his arm. Last year Dooks had been surfing Point Wondai and had come a cropper on the rocks. He'd broken his elbow, leaving it permanently kinked. The same accident had cut his face which had left a ripper of a scar through his top lip. It had sealed his pedigree as a serious surfer.

Suddenly Stride stopped. Dooks wasn't alone. He was talking to a girl, and not just any girl, but *that* girl . . . and she was wearing a wetsuit. So, that's why Dooks wanted his old board, and he'd carried it all the way down here for her! Stride wondered if he should turn around and head back home. Too late.

'Eh,' said Dooks. 'And about time.'

'G'day Dooks,' said Stride, ignoring the girl. 'What's it like in?'

'Not bad, but it was better early this morning – about six – real surfer's time. Where were you? In bed?'

Stride squirmed. Ferd squawked and yanked Stride's hair with his beak. The girl burst out laughing. Stride's cheeks burned.

'Hey!' the girl said. 'I hoped I'd see you today.'

Stride's stomach lurched. He opened his mouth, but she interrupted. 'I brought something for you.' She picked up a bag off her towel, and brought out a handful of mixed birdseed. 'Here, boy,' she crooned.

Stride swallowed . . . uh . . . Ferd, not him.

Ferd behaved like he'd never seen food before and, while he was eating, made soft clucking noises between beakfuls.

'Delicious, eh,' she said scratching the back of Ferd's neck. Ferd stopped eating and shut his eyes in a slow, contented blink. 'And healthy – *mixed* birdseed. Won't make you sick.'

Stride's insides knotted.

'You two met?' Dooks asked surprised.

'Yep.' The girl giggled in that throaty way of hers, eyes on Ferd. 'He prostrated himself before me, but I said I wasn't interested.' She glanced at Stride, smiling.

Dooks looked questioningly at Stride. Stride shook his head and stared out to where the breakers were curling. Right now he wanted to snatch Ferd away like he did last time he met this girl. But the image of her smiling at him like he was a spoilt two-year-old stayed with him.

Dooks broke the silence. 'Wanna hit the surf?'

'Yeah, great.' Stride stopped. Dooks was asking the girl. Stride felt like he'd stumbled into someone else's party.

The girl, her hand still out for Ferd, hesitated, half smiling at Dooks. 'Mmm . . . I haven't surfed much though. I might make a fool of myself.'

Dooks smiled, his lip creasing at the white scar. 'It's a piece a piss, eh, Stride?'

Stride stroked Ferd's back.

The girl ran her toes through the sand then grinned. 'Yeah, okay.'

Dooks was smiling like he never doubted for an instant she would. He passed her the board Stride had brought, running his hands across its surface. 'Could do with a bit of wax . . . I'll zip you.'

She turned, holding up the red dreadlocks, while Dooks zipped up her wetsuit.

'What did you do to your arm?'

'Old surfing injury.'

'Did you break it?'

'Yeah.'

'Ouch.'

'It's cool – carrying a board is much easier with this bend in my arm.'

'That's an impressive scar, too,' she said, turning to get a closer look at his lip. 'Same accident?'

'Yep. Like it? Eight stitches. Pure chick magnet.'

She groaned. 'So wrong.'

Stride thought he might puke. 'I'm off. See ya.'

Dooks didn't turn around. 'See ya. Oh, Stride . . .' He swung in Stride's direction. 'You wanna have a surf after Jess?'

So, her name was Jess.

'Maybe . . .'

Stride urged Ferd onto his shoulder and jogged away along the hard sand at the water's edge. He made for a cluster of seagrass where a sand dune rose. From here he had a clear view of the beach. Dooks was holding Jess around the waist while she stood on the board, showing her what position her feet should be in. Dooks squatted on the sand and leaped to a standing position and then Jess repeated the move a few times.

'Let's get back home, Ferd,' Stride growled, but he didn't move. He watched Jess carry the board into the shallows. As the water deepened, she dropped the board onto the water and slid onto it, paddling over the swell. She ducked her head as she met breaking waves, straightened her arms and pushed herself up to get a view of the next set. Suddenly she swung the board around and paddled furiously. A wave swelled beneath her, picked up momentum, broadened, and then started to thin at the crest. She paddled swiftly and was lifted up and up, then shot forwards as the wave began to arc.

Stride held his breath. Suddenly she leaped to her feet, crouched with her left knee on the board, and then was fully upright, her knees slightly bent. Stride whistled softly: it was a perfect stand; her feet were well positioned, her weight leaning forwards just enough. The wave broke with a roar and she stayed with it, her arms out.

Stride ran down the sand dune. He wanted to yell, tell her how cool it was, how unbelievable it was to catch your very first wave. But he slowed, steadied, stopped himself and walked, remembering he was the uninvited guest.

By the time he got to the wet sand, Jess was walking along the beach, board under her arm, water running off the black slick of her wetsuit.

'Hey,' yelled Dooks. 'That was amazing.'

'Beginner's luck . . . or something.' She smiled and blushed, laying the board on the sand. She reached behind her back for the zip cord.

'What are you doing?' asked Dooks. 'You can't stop now! You've only caught one wave and you're on a roll.'

'No, I've got to go. Dad worries when he thinks I'm outside a fifty metre radius of the camp site.'

Stride frowned. He wanted her to have another go, to see if it was just luck.

'Your dad?' Dooks asked.

'Yeah. During the year I'm with Mum, and then Dad for the holidays. And he's a bit of a stresshead.'

'Oh, okay – what about tomorrow morning when the barrels are really rolling?' asked Dooks.

'Cool.'

'Where's your site? I'll come and get you.'

'It's number thirty-eight – the one with the little purple tent.'

Stride wished he'd walked home when he had the chance. Suddenly Jess turned to him.

'Are you going to have a surf?'

Stride hesitated. He ached to be in the water.

'Scared she'll show you up?' Dooks said, grinning.

Stride stared at him without smiling and unbuttoned his shirt.

'What will you do with him?' Jess turned to Stride, squeezing water out of her hair.

'Who?'

'Your bird.'

Something inside him lurched and his cheeks coloured. How could he have forgotten Ferd?

'Umm . . . Oh . . . I . . .'

'I'll look after him.'

Who did she think she was? No one minded Ferd!

'Uh, he's not used to strangers. He doesn't go to anyone besides me.'

Jess reached over to Ferd who lifted his foot and stepped onto her hand.

Stride gulped. 'Ferd . . .' he croaked. He tried to think of something, anything to say.

'It's okay, old boy,' murmured Jess. 'See, he wants to be with me. Go have a surf.' She smiled at him – a dazzling white smile, a small turned-up nose and the bluest eyes. He couldn't remember seeing eyes so clear.

She scratched Ferd under the beak, while Ferd stretched his neck, silently tapping his tongue on the inner curve of his beak.

Stride wished that something would happen so he could take Ferd back, but no earthquakes split the sand and no tidal waves rose up out of the sea. He undid the leather wristband and handed it over, then realised he would have to do it up for her. Jess held her arm out as if she wasn't attached to it and gently lifted Ferd with her other hand.

'They're sharp, old boy,' she said. Ferd screeched, flapped his wings and lifted his crest, then settled immediately when Jess scratched his head.

'Come up to my site and collect him when you've had enough,' she said.

Stride wished desperately that he'd stayed at home today.

Jess watched the bird on her wrist. Ferd made a soft jangly sound and gazed at her with black eyes.

'Bring the board up to the shop when you're finished,' said Dooks.

Stride made for the surf. He turned back once and saw Jess talking to Dooks, running her hand down

Ferd's long smooth back. He smacked the board down on the foam left by the last outgoing wave and pushed out, paddling wildly.

The waves had become choppy, but Stride enjoyed their unpredictability, and when the sets diminished, he paddled in.

At the surf shop, Dooks was slouching against the railing at the top of the wooden steps that wound down the cliff face to the beach. The upper half of his wetsuit was rolled down; his eyes were shut.

'Eh, Stride,' he said.

'How'd you know it was me?'

'I heard that silly walk that gives you away every time.'

'What walk?'

'Oh you know, that stridey, half walk, half jog thing you do.'

Stride grunted, buttoning his shirt. 'Nah, don't know that I do. Don't think about it really.'

'Guess that's why we call you Stride.'

'I thought it was because my last name is Walker.'

'Nup. How were the waves?'

'Uh, not great . . . But thanks for your board. Should have got it back to you earlier.'

'Well, I thought Jess could use it. She's all right, isn't she? What a surfer! She's better than you mate.' Dooks chuckled.

'Bull! It was beginner's luck.'

'I don't reckon. Nobody's that good first go. Come and see for yourself in the morning. We're going out at six.'

'Nah . . . You two can share the barrels. I just want my bird back.'

Stride jogged by the tide line. He felt incomplete jogging on the beach without Ferd. He missed the weight on his arm, his musky smell, the pleasure he felt at watching Ferd lift his wings in the breeze while he deftly kept his balance, claws firm around Stride's wrist.

He quickly found site thirty-eight. A man sat outside the purple tent in a low beach chair reading the local paper.

'Uh, hi,' Stride said. The man lifted his sunglasses revealing the same startlingly blue eyes as his daughter's. His skin would have been freckled too at one time, but now all the freckles had joined together, giving him a motley tanned look. He smiled.

'Hello, you must be Stride.'

'Uh,' Stride breathed out. 'Yes.'

'I'm Jock, Jess's dad . . . So you're the cockatoo owner?'

'Yeah.' Stride could see he wouldn't have to make any conversation.

'He's a lovely bird. Healthy, well socialised. How long have you had him?'

'He was my dad's bird for about thirty years.'

'Your dad had him from a chick?'

'Yeah, he raised him. We've got photos of when he was young – very ugly.'

'Yes, baby birds are the ugliest of all species I think, other than human.' He chuckled. 'I ran a wildlife shelter for some years. I've seen many. And now he's yours?

Stride squirmed, burrowing one heel into the sand. 'Uh, yeah . . .' A pause hung between them. Stride had to stop himself blurting something to fill the silence. Suddenly the sun felt too hot.

'Is Jess here?' He said it quickly, a pulse throbbing in his neck.

'She just went to the shop for ice-cream. You could wait here if you like. I expect she'll be back shortly.'

'Ah, no thanks. I'll find them.'

'Of course. I'll see you later, Stride.'

'Yeah . . . See you later.' He took a couple of steps, but turned back. 'Oh, just in case I miss her, she could bring Ferd back to my place.' He pointed. 'The white house on the hill. There's a track straight up to it directly behind site eighteen.'

He paused. What was he doing? He'd not only entrusted Ferd to Jess, he'd now told her where he lived and how to find his own private track . . . and he didn't even like her. Next he'd be telling her about the lagoon, the hiding spot on the beach, what nights to look for phosphorescence in the ocean, how the dunes looked in the light of a full moon and that his favourite food was chilli tortillas!

6 The Main Street

The main street was short, with so few shops that Stride expected to see Jess and Ferd straight away. Stride checked the milk bar, the fish and chip shop, the grocers, the hardware store and the op shop. There were several families eating early lunches and thonged campers buying takeaway, but no white cockatoo.

A nervous knot tightened in his belly. What if Jess had let Ferd off his chain, or there'd been some sort of accident? His palms grew damp and a humming sounded in his ears.

He crossed the street, running.

At the real estate office, Stride poked his head inside the door, just in case Jess had wandered in there. The agent was taping For Sale displays in the window. Back out on the street Stride glanced both ways, and then something caught his eye. The poster the agent was putting up in the window advertised a house for sale, but there was something wrong. He blinked and stared.

At first Stride almost laughed. How could they make such a mistake? The house was his house, the Walker house, sitting on its little grassy knoll, its windows reflecting the blue sky, the huge pine to one side. And then another shot – the view of the ocean from the living room, with the caption: 'Superb sea views, right on the foreshore, premier position in Seal Bay, an absolute must-see – a Developer's Dream.'

Stride stood unmoving on the footpath. He watched while the agent carefully taped the poster into place. And then, as though the For Sale notice was the last piece of a jigsaw puzzle, everything slipped into place: keeping the house tidy, washing the walls, Ferd staying outside, his father's clothes tucked into a trunk in the back of the shed . . . and fury rose inside him.

Suddenly the sky seemed to darken, the sea no longer glistened and the golden light of the afternoon faded and Stride felt as though his face glowed fiercely from an internal heat. His heart pounded so loudly, he thought the agent must be able to hear it.

The agent glanced up, saw Stride and cocked his head around the doorway.

'Yes? Can I help you?'

'That house . . . it's not for sale.' He didn't know what else to say. His legs shook and his mouth felt parched as if he'd just eaten a whole packet of dry cereal.

The man suddenly smiled. 'Oh, you're the Walker boy, aren't you? Stride, is it? I'm Herb, Herb Jenkins.' He grinned, but his eyes were fixed solemnly on Stride's face. 'Well, you probably know that anyway – you're a local, we're both dyed-in-the-wool locals, aren't we, Stride?'

The humming in his ears was so loud, Stride was having difficulty hearing.

'Take that poster down. That house isn't for sale.' Stride stared at the poster, refusing to make eye contact with the agent. The shaking in his legs moved up his whole body and he pressed his teeth together to stop them from chattering.

'I know it's difficult to lose a family home. Caroline – your mother – said you –'

'I don't care what *anyone* said, the house isn't for sale – take the poster down.'

'Well, Stride, this is something you'll have to talk

over with your mum. She was in here this morning and she is very keen to sell. Very keen. She said –'

'I don't care what she said.' Stride shouted. 'The house isn't for . . . isn't for sale . . . and no one's moving anywhere!'

Suddenly Stride couldn't talk, all he could feel was an angry blur. The agent's right eye twitched nervously, his mouth smiled and puckered, and the tops of his ears slowly became more pink.

Stride stepped inside and in one sweep, pulled the poster off the window. The next moment, he was running down the footpath, poster in hand, bare feet on the warm concrete. Then across the park, feet gouged by pine cones, between the cypress trees stunted by sea gales, through the straggly line of ti-tree that strayed from the foreshore up the cliff, and back into his own yard.

He doubled over, his chest aching, and fell to the ground, panting, staring at the little white house sitting safely on the knoll where it belonged, where it had been for decades, battered by winter wind and rain, parched by salt and sun in summer, the place he'd always known as his home.

He leaned against the backdoor, while drops of sweat ran down his cheeks, his face pulsed red, and his heart threatened to pound through his chest. In one hand was his crumpled shirt, and in the other, the poster.

He dropped the shirt, squatted and spread the poster over the step and stared at it unbelieving. Then, in slow motion, he tore around the coloured photo of the house. He tore along the roof, up around the chimney, across the top of the pine tree, along the eaves, down the wall, down the short path, around the base of the house, up the wall of the shed, across, around, and back to the house, up to the roof until the house was free of the poster. Then he tore around the words 'Developer's Dream' – around the D over the e and v and e and up over l, over oper's and over D to the end of Dream and back underneath.

Inside he made a collage by using the picture of the house and then sticking the words 'Developer's Dream' across the middle of it. He taped it to the wall of the living room where it'd be seen.

The phone rang.

'Dignam, what happened?'

His mother's voice was high pitched and dangerous. Stride was silent.

'Dignam, Herb is furious. He said you created a furore in the street and ripped the advertisement off the window. Well? Did you?'

'Yes.'

'What were you thinking?'

'What was *I* thinking? What were *you* thinking? When were you going to tell me? Mum?' He paused. 'Does Annie know?'

His mother paused. 'I was going to tell you tonight.'

'So Annie does know. Is that right, Mum?'

'Stride, she's been a lot easier to talk to than you have . . .'

'So I'm the only one who doesn't know!' Stride was yelling now. 'Mum, this is *our* home, our family home. Dad would never have –'

'Dignam!' His mother's voice was fiery and barely controlled, an impending volcano.

Stride wrestled his own voice into a monotone: 'I don't care. Mum, *you* can leave, *you* can do what *you* like, but *I'm* staying in *our* house in Seal Bay. I'm not going anywhere.' He kicked the phone cord from the plug in the wall and let the receiver drop to the floor.

He strode into his room and up-ended his school bag onto the floor where it disgorged pencils, pens, a ruler, two spoons, plastic lunch wrap and a folder. He threw in a T-shirt, drink bottle, cap, wallet, jocks and birdseed, and zipped it up, slipped on some shoes and left the house.

In the shed, he pressed the tyres of his bike. The rear tyre was spongy. He grabbed the bike pump, squatted and pumped furiously.

A sound behind him made him jump, and the pump popped off the tyre, belching a stream of rubbery air.

'Gotcha.'

Stride tried to stand, lost his footing, and fell backwards.

'Jeez!'

It was Jess, almost doubled over laughing.

'Bit edgy, or what?'

Stride struggled up, glaring, his mouth open ready to –

Suddenly he didn't care that she'd surprised him, or that he'd fallen over, or that she was laughing at him. His whole attention was focussed on her bare wrist. For a moment he couldn't speak, he just stood staring at her bare arm. 'Where is he?'

She rubbed the spot where hours earlier Stride had buckled the band.

He stepped forward. 'Where is he?' His voice was low and his eyes were unblinking. 'What have you done with Ferd?'

'Stride,' her face was serious, 'Calm down. I wouldn't have taken him if I couldn't look after him.

I know you adore him . . .' Her voice petered out and her blue eyes stared at him.

'Where is he?' he yelled.

'Your door was open, so I took him inside. He's on the kitchen bench, demolishing an apple.' Her hands were knotted in her pockets.

Stride breathed out, turned back to the bike and squatted to cover the fact that his legs would have buckled had he stayed standing. He leaned his head against the tyre and held onto the spokes until his hands stopped trembling. He reached for the bike pump and reattached it to the valve.

Jess ran the toe of her sandal back and forth through the dust, and then said, 'What's with the bag?' She asked. 'Are you running away?'

Stride grunted as he pumped the tyre.

'I saw what happened in the main street . . .'

Stride unscrewed the bike pump and spat onto his finger, carefully wiping it onto the valve. 'So what?'

'Well . . . I just thought you might want to talk . . .'

'I don't.'

Jess nodded slowly. 'Okay.'

Stride's hands were dusty and streaked with oil. He wiped them on a rag. 'Where were you? I looked everywhere.'

'Well, I went for a walk and then I saw you . . . outside the real estate office.'

He wondered for a moment whether to tell her what it had been about. Instead he said, 'You haven't answered my question.'

'I took Ferd to the lagoon.'

'Oh.'

'It's gorgeous down there, isn't it?' Something in the way she tilted her head made him pause.

'Um . . . yeah.'

'It's one of your favourite places, isn't it?'

He didn't answer, but put the pump back onto the shelf.

He swung around suddenly. 'You were at the lagoon yesterday! That was you, wasn't it . . . Ferd saw you too.' He watched her, carefully.

Jess grinned.

'Maybe.' She paused and leaped at a low beam, hung and swung her legs up, her toes to the beam. She twisted her head back and looked at him upside down. 'Hey, you haven't answered my question either – are you running away?'

'I can't talk to you when you're doing that.'

Jess stopped and steadied herself. She giggled, her nose wrinkling slightly and started swinging again, dropping her head back and laughing, her mouth wide.

Stride shook his head and sighed. 'No, I'm not running away. I'm going to my Gramp's house.' He squatted, picked up a stick and squiggled it in the dirt.

'Oh, okay.' Jess let go of the beam. 'What about Ferd? Are you taking him?'

'He comes with me everywhere.' He said it quickly. 'He'd fret without me . . . probably wouldn't eat . . . could get sick . . .'

Jess smiled 'You're scared.'

Stride stood up. 'Of what?' He said it too quickly, too loudly, too forcefully.

'See. You know you are.'

He turned back to the bike, pressing a tyre. 'You're full of it.'

'You're scared of losing Ferd. You're scared he'll like someone else more than you . . . I bet you're too scared to let him go.'

Stride felt the same dislocating blur of rage he'd felt earlier. 'How would you know!' he yelled. 'You know nothing about me.'

Jess's smile faded. She stared at him with her pale, blue eyes, her hands jammed into her back pockets. 'Sorry. It's none of my business. I shouldn't have said anything.' She pushed her hair back. 'Thanks for trusting me to mind Ferd. I really enjoyed having him. Um . . . I guess you won't be surfing in the morning?'

Stride looked away, unable to say anything.

He pressed the other bike tyre, picked up the bag he'd dropped and swung it onto his back.

The light through the shed door was muzzled as a bank of grey cloud rose from the west, obscuring the sun.

'No,' he said, now trusting himself to speak. 'No, I won't be.'

She opened her mouth, closed it, and then said, 'When are you coming back?'

Stride shrugged and wheeled the bike out onto the driveway, kicking down the stand.

'Dunno.'

'Well . . .' Jess hesitated. 'Uh, I'll see you later then.'

Stride stomped inside to get Ferd. Through the window he saw her hesitate, just before she disappeared into the trees. She turned toward the house and lifted her hand in a wave.

7 Gramps

Stride's mood lifted as he pedalled out of town. Ferd was perched on the handlebars, his head thrust forward, his wings raised, his crest up, screeching. The bank of cumulus cloud had edged south and the sun was hot again, and Stride was soon drenched in sweat.

He could still smell the sea, but before long the saltiness was lost as the forest greened and thickened around him. It grew cooler under the towering gums and Stride breathed in the bush, heavy with the scent of eucalyptus. The heat of the last month had altered the forest. The soft lime tendrils of the tree ferns had darkened and toughened and the undergrowth was brown. In the light breeze, Stride heard the change. The voice of the foliage had grown harsher, raspy.

His legs pumped furiously, until at last, he rounded the final bend and saw the old farm, with its wooden gate propped upright, the hinges rusty and unmoving. The long grass in the paddocks moved stiffly on drying stalks.

This was where his dad had grown up and where he'd found Ferd as an ugly bald chick. Stride had heard the story from when he was little. He remembered a Sunday night when he was on his dad's boat. His mum and Annie had driven to Melbourne for an art exhibition opening, so Stride and his dad had taken a boys' trip on the boat. His dad had turned out the lamp and a half moon reflected off the water, making silver shapes shimmer on the ceiling of the cabin. Ferd was perched on his dad's shoulder and had settled so low that his feet were almost invisible beneath his feathers. His eyes were shut and he occasionally emitted small 'crrk' sounds, opened his eyes and shut them again.

'How old were you when you got Ferd?' Stride and his dad had finished playing Snap! and Uno and were sipping strong sweet tea.

Frank blew on his tea, his hands around the tin mug.

'Probably about ten or eleven . . . it was the year I was in grade six.'

'Where did he come from?'

Frank's eyes softened as he smiled at Stride through the steam from his mug. Stride pushed back against the seat.

'Well, an old nesting stag had fallen into the wetlands at home – at Gramps and Gran's farm. I don't know how many babies there were, but when I found them, there was a dead one and one that was just alive. There could have been others, I don't know. At first I didn't see the living one – he was huddled in a clump of sedge. He was prickly with sprouting feathers, and he was frightened and weak. I carried him home inside my coat. His beak was oversized for a bird so small and he kept opening and shutting it expecting food. I had to find out what food to give him, and then I had to feed him regularly through the day and set my alarm at night. He was a hungry little fella. Feisty too!'

'Did you get tired?'

'Not too bad . . . it must have been in the holidays I think.'

'Did Gramps help?'

'Gran gave me a bit of a hand, but they left it up to

me mainly. That's what I wanted. I wanted to feel he was really my pet.'

'What did you feed him?'

'It was a mixture of chicken pellets, rolled oats and crushed sunflower seeds.'

'How did you feed it to him?'

'Oh, I mashed it all together with water, sometimes spit, until it was soft, and pushed it into his mouth with my fingers.'

'Spit? Yuck!'

'Yeah, what's a bit of spit between friends, eh boy?' Frank turned and scratched Ferd's chest. Ferd opened his eyes and stretched a wing.

'He grew fast . . .' Frank sipped his tea and gazed out through the porthole. 'And then he was big enough to eat birdseed.'

'When did he get feathers?'

'That happened pretty fast too – can't remember exactly how long. But when he had a full coat of feathers, I thought he should start to fly. So we'd go out together and practise flying.'

'With you riding your bike?'

'Yeah, that was later, though. First, when he was learning, I'd put him on the ground and walk away from him and he'd half hop, half fly after me. Then I put him on low branches and move away. We'd go through the same thing. And we kept going over and over it until he got the hang of it. Sometimes I used to climb up into the tree with him on my shoulder and put him on a high branch and then jump down. He'd follow me, first hopping from branch to branch and then he'd fly from branch to branch and then glide all the way down. Then when he could do that, we'd do the bike thing and he'd lift off the handlebars and fly alongside.'

Stride sat back and stared over the silvery water, picturing the little boy in grey shorts he'd seen in old home movies at Gramps and Gran's.

'And he followed you around all the time?'

'When we were in the house he'd pigeon-toe around behind me, doing that talking out the side of his beak like he does.'

Stride giggled. 'Yeah . . .'

'Anyway, time for bed – early start tomorrow. You have to bunk down matey,' he said to Stride and, 'Onto your perch Ferd.' Ferd gave a 'crrk' of protest, but stepped onto the perch Frank had constructed beside his bunk.

Then Stride had crawled into his sleeping bag and drifted to sleep to the rock of the boat, the 'ting, ting' of the rigging against the mast, the 'bllp, bllp' of water against the timber, and his dad's snoring.

Outside the moon sailed westward and slowly faded as daylight came.

Ferd screeched. He always made a special sound whenever they came to Gramps's farm. He held his head up, his crest high, his eyes alert.

'What is it, boy? Got some relatives near?' Stride brushed his hand down Ferd's back and rode through the gate and past the old vegie patch. It used to grow enough to feed them all, but was slowly reduced in size as Gramps and Gran grew too old to manage a big garden. Then Gran had died two years ago and now Gramps grew just enough tomatoes and cucumbers and beans for himself.

There was a chook pen, the red chooks sunning their outstretched wings, kicking dust over their feathers as they lay in little dirt nests they'd hollowed out along the fence. And there was the farmhouse, settled on a low ridge that curved down to a grassy wetland. The old house looked more tired than when he was here for Christmas, just weeks ago. The unpainted weatherboards folded around the house, cupping sagging window frames and bending beneath the tilting verandah. The rusty patchwork of corrugated iron sheets on the roof merged into one shimmering plate, ticking with the heat.

Stride's gut lurched at the sight of Gramps framed in the dark doorway – an old man in overalls with a worn leather belt and one broken shoulder strap attached by hay band to the buckle. He waved and yelled, 'Hi Gramps.'

Stride pedalled to where the steps leading up to the verandah used to be, lifted Ferd off the bike and set him onto the verandah. He pushed his bike against a post and vaulted onto the porch, smelling the damp air from the wetlands, the scent of the sea now left behind.

'Hey, mate,' said Gramps, and smiled, his leathery skin forming thick folds around his brown eyes. Stride hugged him.

'You knew I was coming?'

'Well, your mother rang. She guessed you might come here, so I've been keeping my eyes on the drive-way.'

Stride sniffed and swung his bag off his back.

'Mum rang? Did she tell you?'

Gramps didn't answer, but took Stride's bag and led the way into the old kitchen.

'What time did you leave?'

'About 2.45.'

Gramps checked his watch. 'Well, that was one of your best times. You must have been pedalling pretty fast.'

Stride grinned. 'Yeah, the legs are a bit sore. How long did I take?'

'Well, you beat your record by two and a half minutes, but I'm afraid I'm all out of hundreds and thousands.'

Stride's grin broadened. Gramps used to time him when he was four years old and had just taken off his training wheels. He'd ride to the end of the driveway and back, trying to beat his record. Gramps would sprinkle hundreds and thousands on his grimy little palm if he beat his record and Stride would lick them off, tasting sugar, salt, and the perishing rubber of his bike handles.

They sat at the laminex table drinking lemon cordial.

'Going to stay for a while, Diggy?'

Gramps was the only person in the world who called him Diggy. If anyone else tried it he would probably want to slug them, but with Gramps it was okay.

Stride massaged his calves with one hand. 'Yeah.

Need to clear my head.' He wanted to talk about the house, but he wasn't sure how Gramps would react. He drew a line with his finger through a puddle of spilt cordial.

'Did you know, Gramps?'

Ferd strolled pigeon-toed around the table, grumbling in a soft voice that there was nothing for him to eat. Stride pulled a handful of seed from his pocket and left a trail across the end of the table.

'Know what, Diggy?'

'Did Mum tell you?'

'What's that, Diggy?'

'About the house, our house?'

Gramps stroked Ferd's feathers gently.

'Yes, I know now . . . Your mum just told me.'

Stride continued to run his finger through the cordial, but his eyes were on Gramp's face.

'Well?'

'Diggy, your dad loved that place. Gran and I helped him find it. But it was his choice of home, not your mum's. I think she wants to move to a bigger town . . . or . . . somewhere new . . .'

'But why didn't she tell me? She told Annie and she didn't tell me – I had to find out for myself. It's a bugger of a way to find out.' He paused . . . he'd never sworn in front of Gramps. 'She should have discussed it with both of us at the same time.'

'Yes, she should have.' Gramps said it quietly, almost under his breath. He slowly picked up the glasses, carried them to the sink and wiped the table. 'Would you like to take a dip in the dam?'

Stride sighed and pushed the damp hair off his face. 'Yeah.'

Stride leaped off the verandah. It was attached to the swaying garage where Gramps's Holden was parked. When Stride was young, he had waited, excited, at the kitchen window for the old car to turn down the driveway when Gramps and Gran came for Sunday dinner.

'Dad, they're coming,' he'd call as it nosed slowly through the gate.

Sunday lunch was the only meal of the week that his dad prepared, and it was always the same: a roast, followed by baked apples and ice-cream for dessert.

'Why doesn't Mum cook for Gramps and Gran?' Stride had asked as he helped press stuffing into the cored apples.

'Your mum's not the only chef in this house, you know, and anyway, they're my parents, so I cook,' Frank had said and swung him up onto the bench next to Annie where he could suck the apple cores and coil the peeled apple skin around his wrist. 'And Mum needs some time for her drawing – otherwise she gets a bit cranky, and then we all suffer,' he'd said with a chuckle.

Early Sundays, Mum tucked her sketchpad and her wooden pencil case into a canvas bag and took off towards the lagoon.

'Back for lunch?' Dad would call through the kitchen window.

'Probably,' she'd call over her shoulder.

But sometimes she'd lose track of time and wouldn't get back until the baked apples were being served.

Stride hadn't seen Gramps behind the wheel of the old car for months now. He wondered if it would still start, if the battery was any good.

He followed the course of the valley, where in winter and during spring rains, a small creek flowed into the dam. At the bottom of the valley were the wetlands and the embankment that formed the dam.

It was overgrown with regrowth and small blue wrens teetered on spindly legs and darted in and out of the low vegetation, chirping with shrill persistent voices. One side of the dam was shaded by a giant white gum. Lengths of bark had slithered from its trunk into the water where they lay beneath the surface, lurking like stringy water beasts.

Stride tethered Ferd to a tree stump at the water's edge, stripped off and waded in. Although he knew the dam well, the deep spots, the old submerged logs, the yabby holes, he entered warily, knowing the storms of last winter may have washed change beneath the surface.

As always, the upper layer was lukewarm, but lower down it was cold enough to send his skin into gooseflesh. He dove deeply to where vision was reduced to a skulking brown and the cold water sucked the heat out of him.

As he broke the surface, everything was still except for the sound of his gasping breath in the dry noon heat. He floated for a while, then, treading water, watched the clearing sky through the eucalyptus leaves that hung like grey-green daggers. Brown algae rose silently from the disturbed depths speckling his skin. The dusky smell filled his nostrils. Dam water: old and secret, resurrecting childhood. He and Annie used to swim down here often.

'Have you heard of a Whoompla?' she'd asked him one hot afternoon as they sat in the shallows, stirring up the mud with their feet.

'Don't be silly,' he'd said. 'There's no such thing.'

'There is. It has a jelly eye and a waving mouth. If you get too close – whoomp – you're gone, swallowed in one gulp.'

He'd stared at her, his mouth open.

'And,' she'd continued in a whisper, 'there's a Whoompla living at the bottom of the dam.'

He'd gasped. 'That's not true,' he'd squeaked. He'd leaped up and run back to the house, leaving his towel on the bank.

'The Whoompla isn't interested in pipsqueaks like you,' Frank had whispered to him as he sat on his lap trickling dam water down his legs. 'I used to swim in the dam every summer and the Whoompla wasn't interested in me either. But, if I swam there now . . .' he patted his belly, '*that* might be a different thing altogether.'

Stride had reported his father's response to Annie, his big blue eyes glowing. 'See!' he'd said, 'You don't know everything!' And he'd gazed up at Frank like he was all-knowing, all-powerful.

Stride's skin had prickled with horror, though, and

he'd promised himself he would never let his dad swim in the dam, no matter how immortal he seemed.

And then last summer, the three of them had swum there for the first time in ages.

'Remember the Whoompla?' Stride had said.

'You believed every word I told you, Stride,' Annie had said. 'You were so gullible.' And she'd jumped on his shoulders and tried to duck him, and between her and Frank, they got him under.

Stride squelched through the mud up onto the bank and sat naked, the sun on his back, water dripping on his shoulders from his hair, enjoying the chill of the air on wet skin.

And then strangely, everything seemed too quiet, too still, too alone.

He flicked the water off, dressed, lifted Ferd who made a dive at his knuckle for being so long, and walked back to the house.

Stride was woken by a flock of white cockatoos kicking up a racket in the spreading branches of the eucalypts west of the house. He wondered if they were fighting, and if so, over what – favourite branches, food? And if they weren't fighting, what were they telling each other – rich feeding grounds, gossip, weather forecasts?

Stride watched Ferd sitting on the windowsill, gnawing at the putty at the base of the glass, talking in his 'conversation voice' as he dropped nibbled putty onto the sheet. Stride wondered what it was like for Ferd to be back at Gramps's farm. Did he remember that his family lived here? Did he miss his flock, his freedom . . .

Already the room was hot and Stride was sweating in the narrow bed his dad used to sleep in as a child. Beyond the double-hung sash window the sky was cloudless. A bluish haze was building above the euca-lypts as heat drew the oil from the leaves into the still air.

This was the room his dad and his brother had shared until they had left home, and Stride wondered how they'd survived, cramped into this small space, with its dark Baltic pine boards lining the walls and high ceiling.

He tugged hard on the metal loops attached to the window frame, hoping – but he knew the window was impossible to open as it had been painted shut long ago.

Thoughts of home flickered through his mind. He had images of prospective buyers lining up at the door, eager to see the cottage they intended to bulldoze. Men in suits busily tapping figures into calculators. Women with briefcases estimating the cost of the view. Children stickybeaking in his bedroom, staring out his window to the beach, playing in his ti-tree tunnel. His palms prickled.

His mother had rung for him last night, but he had refused to talk to her.

'She's your mother, Diggy. You should speak to her,' Gramps had said.

'She had no right to do what she did,' growled Stride.

'Diggy!'

'I don't care, Gramps,' Stride had said. 'I don't want to talk to her. She didn't tell me because she knew I'd hate the idea.'

'She's been through a lot this last four months.'

'And I haven't?' He'd said it loudly, angrily.

'Diggy, it's hard for everyone.'

'Gramps, I have to say how I feel. I know you don't like to, but I have to speak my mind.'

Gramps had watched him silently, nodding slightly. 'Well, Diggy, I won't tell you what to do, but be careful that you don't say anything you'll regret. Scars take a long time to heal and sometimes it's wiser not to say anything.'

There was something in the way Gramps had spoken that made Stride pause.

'What do you mean, Gramps? Is there something . . . ' he stopped, not quite knowing what to say, and then he'd blurted: 'What scars?'

Gramps had folded his newspaper and softly tapped it against his leg.

'Well, Diggy, your dad met your mother in Melbourne – she was a city girl – and he brought her up here. Your dad stayed in Seal Bay for lots of reasons. He was a fisherman of course, but there're much richer fishing grounds than those along this part of the coast. He could have gone to any one of the villages to the north. He was also very fond of the old house over-looking the sea, but most of all, he stayed where he could keep an eye on your grandma and me. I know it wasn't what your mother wanted. She had had her own painting studio in Melbourne, but your dad could be stubborn . . . I think your mum felt it was your gran and me who were to blame for your dad not leaving Seal Bay.

'So maybe now, Diggy, your mum is doing something she's always wanted to do.' Gramps had put his hand on Stride's shoulder and they hadn't spoken for the rest of the evening.

Stride had sat on the edge of the bed. Light from the kitchen made a diagonal of yellow on the floor outside his door. So was that why mum's painting trips on Sundays were so long, why dad always prepared Sunday lunch, why she often failed to make trips to the farm? He'd stroked Ferd's back and lit the candle that stood on the bookshelf by the bed. The flame grew tall and then receded, nodding gently in an unseen current of air. He watched the small yellow beacon while, outside, frogs from the wetlands sent a chorus of notes into the night. He'd pinched out the flame and lay in the darkness, until sleep came.

He could hear Gramps in the kitchen making tea – the jug boiling, the clink of the teapot. He could smell toast and knew Gramps would be spreading it with butter, thick enough to melt into pools, with jam made from the blackberries that grew in vigorous thickets behind the garage.

The cockatoos were silent now and the roof expanded in the heat – chink, chink, chink.

Stride tried the window again – everything felt stifling: the still unmoving trees, the ticking cottage, the tranquillity of the wetlands, even the cup of tea Gramps was pouring. The habitual tasks Gramps performed. They somehow obligated him to be grateful, to be good, to be responsible. He took a deep breath, and then another, fearful that in this little room, he would suddenly be unable to breathe.

He had to get back to the beach, with the sea out his window, the moist salty air. And he had stuff to sort out – the house thing, his mum, Annie.

He threw off the sheet, pulled on shorts and tossed his few belongings into his bag.

In the kitchen, Gramps had poured tea for two. His gnarled hands, permanently stained, shook as he placed cups on saucers.

'How did you sleep, Diggy?'

For an instant, Stride wanted to rush to him, hold his hands, touch the leathery cheeks, tell him . . . tell him . . . tell him that everything was all right. But the feeling faded as he realised how much he'd wanted Gramps to take the role of a dad – strong and willing to fight, for him and Annie to keep the old house. Something heavy held his feet and his energy slipped through the cracked linoleum. He stayed where he was, murmuring that he had slept fine, without looking at Gramps.

They ate breakfast and drank their tea. Stride cleared the table, wanting to make amends for the silence.

'Is there anything I can do for you, Gramps, before I go? Anything outside . . . some mowing?' He tried to sound enthusiastic, but it was wooden and forced.

Gramps took a deep breath. 'Don't worry, Diggy. Your Uncle Lenny is due the day after tomorrow. He brings his ride-on mower and gets it done in no time. My old mower . . . The blade's are blunt and trying to start it . . . mmm . . . it's a bit of a stinker to get going.'

Stride nodded.

'Anyway, might be a bit cooler by then,' Gramps continued. 'Always a bit cautious about sparks from the mower in such hot conditions. Bad fire day today.'

Silence slid between them once more. Ferd, roosting on the kitchen door, screeched intermittently. What would happen to Gramps if he got sick or he had to get off the property in a hurry? He had no close neighbours and the old place was almost untenable now. Uncle Lenny could mow lawns and clean gutters, but he was an accountant – he wasn't practical like Stride's dad. He couldn't fix the fence, or replace the screen door. He didn't have a clue about the septic tank system.

'Gramps, do you ever think you ought to leave here and move into a retirement home or something?'

'Eh?' Gramps was frowning.

'You know – the farm's so big, and the house needs lots of work.'

'Don't you start, Diggy. I just had the same conversation with your Uncle Lenny. He wants me to sell.'

'Does he?'

'Yes, but I'm not interested. All my best memories are here. I'm not leaving.'

'But you're here on your own. What if something happens?'

'I'm okay. I've got the phone and I've got the old Holden.'

'Is it still going?'

'I'll have a tinker with it. I know it inside out and back to front.'

'It's pretty old now, Gramps.'

'Diggy, I'm all right. Stop worrying . . . and don't say anything to your mum. She's got enough on her mind.'

Stride sighed. 'Okay, Gramps.' He gazed out the window. The room was hot. 'Gramps, I think I'll ride home before it gets any hotter.'

'Yes, Diggy, do that . . .' Gramps murmured. 'Give me two rings so I know you're home safe.'

On the verandah, Stride swung his bag onto his back and hauled his bike into position. Ferd screeched from inside, flew down onto the floor behind them and wig-wagged his way out the door to Stride where he jumped onto his foot, up onto his bent knee, then thigh and pulled himself onto Stride's shoulder holding his T-shirt in his beak.

Stride put his arm around Gramps, gave him a quick hug, straddled his bike, clicked Ferd's chain on, and sped down the driveway.

He turned and waved. A heaviness threatened to settle on him seeing Gramps silhouetted on the oddly angled verandah, the old brick chimney reaching to the early morning sky behind him.

The road stretched ahead, empty and inviting. The weight hovered until the smell of the sea became sharp in his nostrils, and then lifted, and he felt he could ride forever.

8 Truce

At home, all was still. There were no queues of prospective buyers, no real estate agents, not even his mother or Annie, and the torn For Sale poster he'd stuck to the wall was gone.

Stride pushed open the door to his room. It had been tidied. His bed was made, his books were evenly placed in the book shelf, the rubbish bin was empty, the computer desk had only a computer on it, his shoes were in a row, paired, the floor was vacuumed and his clothes hung neatly in the wardrobe, all with coat-hangers facing the same way. After years of work at Point Wondai's only clothes shop, no one could fold a jumper or hang a shirt as well as his mum.

'Well, Ferd, no prizes for guessing who's been in my room . . . tidying it for a stupid developer who won't care less what the house is like because he'll knock it down and build units!'

Within seconds he had flipped his bag upside down, spilling clothes and birdseed onto the carpet. He pulled the doona off his bed and opened all the drawers wide. He sat on the stripped bed with a small smile.

'That's more like home, eh, Ferd?'

Ferd jumped off the bed onto the floor for the spilt birdseed, and Stride lay back on his bed and sighed.

'Good to be home, Ferd?' The only sound was the cracking of corn kernels.

When the phone rang, Ferd squawked, lifted his wings and flapped into the living room where he climbed up the back of the couch – beak, claw, beak, claw – and settled on the headrest.

Stride's heart was beating fast. What if a buyer was ringing to enquire about the house, or if the agent wanted to show someone through? What would he say? That the house wasn't for sale, and even if it was, who'd buy it, with its unstable sandy foundations, its cracking walls, its . . .

'Hello . . . Oh, Gramps, sorry. I forgot to ring . . .
Sorry . . . Okay . . . Thanks . . . Bye.'

He hung up, stared vacantly at the phone, sighed and
turned to Ferd who was looking at him questioningly.

'Ferd!' Stride yelled. Ferd had pooped on the back
of the couch. 'Ferd, just cos I trash my room, doesn't
mean you can make a mess.' He grabbed a cloth and
swiped at the grey mess. Ferd made a dive at Stride with
an open beak and angry crest.

'Yeah, I know. I don't like Mum cleaning up my
stuff and you don't like me cleaning up yours, but
unless you learn how to do it yourself, I have to. Come
on, let's eat and get out of here – time for the beach.'

He spread butter on slices of bread with slabs of
cheese and pushed them together in a sandwich.

Outside, the temperature had started to soar. A wind
had risen – a hot drying northerly. Stride thought about
going to the beach via the main street to check the real
estate agent's window, but just the idea of it made his
gut churn.

Annie. He needed to speak to her. Back inside he
grabbed the phone. She worked part-time at Simone's
Milk Bar.

'Hi, it's Stride, is Annie there? Hi . . . Can you get a
minute off to talk? Okay, see you soon.'

Annie was sitting at an outdoor table with two milk-shakes in tumblers, drops of condensation running down the glass.

'Better be chocolate or I won't drink it.'

She turned at his voice. 'How could I forget straw-berry milkshake tantrums? Of course it's chocolate.' She looked up at him, shading her eyes.

Stride pulled out a chair. He avoided her eyes, while he drank his milkshake. She ran her fingers slowly through the beads of water on the rippled glass. Stride wiped his mouth with the back of his hand and frowned at her. She popped the bubbles on the top of her drink with the end of her straw.

'Why didn't you tell me?'

'I'm sorry, I . . .'

'I thought we told each other everything.'

'Just wait . . . you don't know the whole story.'

'Well, what is the whole story?'

'I overheard Mum talking on the phone to the agent. And when I asked her about it, she made me promise not to tell you.'

'Great. Thanks.' He pushed his fringe out of his

eyes with the back of his hand and stared out over the bay.

'She wanted to tell you herself.'

'Well, she wussed out.'

Annie sighed, 'She was waiting for the right time.'

'So when was the right time? When a bulldozer was flattening my bedroom?'

'She made a mistake. Got her timing wrong.'

Stride studied the sea. His belly knotted. The surf was calm, although the northerly had started to raise some whitecaps down the far end of the bay.

'Drink the rest of your milkshake or I'll have it.' Annie and Stride eyed each other.

'Never,' he said.

Annie put her straw to her lips and blew a stream of milk over Stride. He leaned across the table and grabbed for the straw. She pushed her chair back out of his reach. He jumped up and swung her seat back at an angle.

'Truce!' she squealed.

Stride released her seat and sat down. He swiped the milk off his face and neck with the back of his hand.

'Yeah well, next time, tell me, especially when it's such a huge thing.'

'Okay.' Annie ran her fingers up Ferd's neck lifting his crest.

'Cccrk.'

'You! You'd agree with anything he said.'

'Ccrk.'

'Stride, I'm really sorry . . .'

'Yeah. Just back me up tonight when I tackle mum about selling?'

Annie folded her arms and put her head to one side. 'I don't want to leave our house – I love it. But I don't want a huge fight. Let's try to deal with it the way Dad would have?'

Stride smiled. 'Yeah, okay. I'll say what I think, but try to stay calm, like Dad . . .'

'Deal.'

Annie stood. 'I gotta get back to work. See you later this afternoon. Where you off to?'

'Oh, around.'

'You should get a job.'

'Yeah.'

9 Tension

'Mum, he can't stay there on his own.' Stride waved his fork in the air. Ferd was perched on the back of the chair with a piece of apple in his claw held up to his beak. 'The old place is going to fall down on top of him,' he gestured with the fork, 'or he could have a fall . . . or . . . or . . . a stroke or something, and no one would know.'

His mum sat with her arms folded on the table, her untouched plate pushed aside.

'I've got enough to think about at the moment.'

'Well, he didn't want me to say anything because he knows you've got a lot on your mind, but I think Gramps should be high on the list.'

'Leave it, Dignam. I just can't think about it right now.' She unfolded her arms and picked up her fork.

'How long is it since he's driven the old Holden? I'll bet it won't even start now. He couldn't even get off the property if he needed to . . .'

'Dignam,' her voice had risen. 'I'm sure you're right, but you're hardly in any position to start dictating what I should or shouldn't do. Your behaviour of late has been immature to say the least. The situation with the agent . . .'

'Yes, Mum, the agent.' Stride could feel heat rising above the neck of his T-shirt. He glanced at Annie. She was looking down at her food. He swallowed, coughed and let his fork rest on his plate. He ran his other hand down Ferd's back and silently rehearsed the conversation he'd had with Annie at the milk bar.

'Annie and I think it was really . . . um . . . unfair that you didn't discuss the whole house business with us before you went to an agent. In fact, it was . . .' Stride's voice was gathering momentum. Annie coughed. Stride glanced at her. She mouthed something behind her hand. Stride swung back on his chair, slid his hands through his hair, righted his chair, ran a finger across Ferd's feet, and started again. Ferd continued nibbling the apple.

'What I mean is, I think it's important for us to make big decisions together.'

Annie gave him a thumbs up under the table. Stride looked across at his mother. She was pushing a lettuce leaf around her plate with her fork.

'I'm sorry, Stride. I didn't think the agent would act on it so quickly. I thought I would have cleared it with you two before he started advertising. So I am sorry you had to find out that way. It wasn't appropriate.' She concentrated on the wedge of tomato she had just stabbed.

'So what happens now?'

'Well, perhaps we should talk about it.'

'We are talking about it, and we don't want to leave.' Stride's voice had gone up half an octave. Annie kicked him under the table and Ferd squawked and dropped his apple skin onto the floor.

'Oh, Stride. I can't afford to fix it. It's old. Old houses gobble up money. Any builder will tell you that. As soon as you work on one section, another section falls apart. Builders can't give accurate quotes because they don't know the cost themselves until they start taking down walls.'

'But the house is fine the way it is. We don't need to change it.'

'There are huge cracks on the south wall.'

'They just need to be rendered.'

'And the chimney leaks.'

'It's always done that.'

'And the tin on the roof lifts in high winds.'

'That's not hard to fix.'

'The nail holes are rusted through – the whole roof needs replacing.'

'That's do-able.'

'Stride – you're not being practical. It's a huge and expensive proposition.'

'It's been okay for the last fifteen years. How come, all of a sudden, it isn't okay?'

'It's not "all of a sudden". It's something that happens gradually. You can keep on ignoring it, or wait until it falls down. If we sell now, then at least we'll get a reasonable price.'

Stride lost hold of his father's calm. 'Mum, that's rubbish – this house will be bulldozed whether we sell it now or in ten years time. Nobody wants this old place. Not even you. Only Annie and I want it. And Dad. He would never have agreed to this.' He banged the table with his fists and veins stood out in narrow blue tunnels down his temples. Ferd rose off the chair and flew to the top of Stride's bedroom door where he screeched and threw up his crest. He watched them at the table, tilting his head from side to side.

Stride's mother stood up. 'Stride – it was a very hard decisions. I'm trying to work out what is best for us financially. Of course it would be different if your dad was here, but he's not. I have to support you two. I can't be sentimental. This is where you grew up, so of course you're very attached to it. But everything's changed now. I need you to try to understand. We got off to a bad start with this whole agent thing and I'm very sorry, as I said. Let's talk about it again when we've both cooled down.'

Annie sighed and pushed back her chair. Stride could feel her glare on the back of his neck as she picked up her plate and put it in the sink.

'I'm going to Soula's, Mum – I'll see you later.'

'You're on dishes tonight, Annie.' Mum's voice was tired. She sat forward in her chair and rested her chin in her hand. Stride saw a fine web of wrinkles on the side of her neck that he'd never noticed before.

'Just leave them in the sink – I won't be long,' said Annie.

'I'll do them.' Stride's voice was low. 'Pay back for the chocolate milkshake.'

Annie stared at him without smiling.

Stride grimaced and looked away. He'd blown it.

10 The Lagoon

Down on the beach the next morning, Stride scanned the water. He wondered if Dooks and Jess had surfed yesterday. If he hadn't gone to Gramps's, he might have surfed with them. Maybe that would have been better than sweating it out at the old farm. He would have seen if Jess could repeat her performance on the board; they might have talked, maybe he could have told her why he went to the farm. No, Dooks would have been there, and he would have been the hanger-on.

Ferd squawked and Stride saw he was nearly at Jess's tent. He stopped, wondering if she was there. He could ask her about . . . about . . . well, about doing something, something together. His stomach somersaulted at the thought and sweat needled his palms. In that same instant, he pictured her, laughing, her blue eyes bright and piercing. And, 'You're scared to let him go . . .' He turned sharply toward the lagoon, and burst into a sprint before slowing to an easy jogging pace.

At the sand dunes, Stride ran diagonally, his arm held high, Ferd's claws around his wrist. His feet squeaked and slid on the dry sand and, looking over his shoulder, he watched the wind of his solitary footsteps on the silver slope.

The sheltered lagoon was still. Stride shoved his thongs into his shorts pockets and waded into the amber water up to his waist, sinking ankle deep in sand. Holding Ferd aloft, he ducked his head and rose, his hair and face streaming.

'Pity you're not a swimmer, Ferd. The water's fantastic.' Ferd nibbled Stride's hair, and tamped his tongue against the inside of his beak. Stride cupped his hand and Ferd dipped his head and drank, straightening up to swallow. He repeated it twice more and then settled back on Stride's shoulder, murmuring through closed beak.

Suddenly Ferd swung around, squawked and threw his crest forward, his eyes wide. Stride followed his gaze and was conscious again of the feeling of being watched. But as before, he could see no one. He waded to the far side of the lagoon and scrambled up the bank. Again Ferd shrieked and lifted off Stride's arm, flying as high as he could.

On an overhanging branch, Stride saw the grey leathery shape of a young goanna stretched the length of the limb. It was watching them and quite still, but for its tongue lashing slowly in and out as if tasting what this new disturbance might be. Ferd landed on Stride's head, squawking. Stride gently lifted him down, stroking his crest until Ferd was calm and silent. They stood for a moment staring together at the lizard's dusty folds, then moved into the trees.

Here ti-tree grew thickly and the undergrowth of coral fern and sword grass made progress difficult. Stride thought he heard something above the harsh metallic hum of cicadas, and goose bumps rose along his wet arms and at the back of his neck. He felt a shudder of fear. He had never felt afraid at the lagoon before – it was his safe haven. He turned, but all was undisturbed – the trees were still, transfixed by the heat, the dunes rose high behind them with the line of his own footprints curving in an arc down to the water's edge.

Just then the breeze picked up, a searing offshore

wind. Stride thought he could smell something. No, it was gone. Ferd screeched, agitated. Stride felt fear creeping from his belly up into his throat.

Then there was a clear, shrill sound that spiralled above the cicadas like a siren above traffic noise. Stride felt his heartbeat quicken and he strained to listen beyond the voomp voomp in his ears.

There it was again: a scream piercing the hot air. He turned in the direction of the lagoon. When it came again, it wasn't a wordless scream, it was someone calling for help, and not just calling for help, but calling his name.

'Stride! Help!'

Sweat ran down his hands and face and his shirt stuck to his back. Heat pulsed through him.

He gulped, tried to yell in return, his voice faltered and he tried again. 'Where are you?' It sounded pitiful, insignificant. For the first time in his life he felt disconnected from the bush – it was a stranger to him.

He called again, but there was no response.

He pushed forward, but his legs were leaden as if wet sand clung in clumps to his thongs, and they trembled against the tangle of wiregrass. He tripped, his foot caught in a loop of the trailing vine-like grass.

He grunted, untangling himself with uncertain hands. Overhead the sky had become brassy and the air pressed heavily against him.

'Stride.'

He stopped abruptly. The voice came from somewhere close, low down.

'Jess?' She was squatting at the base of a banksia, only two metres away, her face strangely white, her freckles stark against her pale skin. She was staring up at him, her eyes frozen with fear.

'What's wrong?' He stopped as she pointed. The tail of a snake, black with a red line at belly level, slid, oiled and soundless into the undergrowth. Stride stared at the place where it had disappeared. There was no more movement, nothing, as if there hadn't been anything there at all.

'I . . . I . . . didn't see it. I nearly stepped . . .' Her voice broke and she lowered her head onto her knees, her arms wrapped around her legs. She was shaking. 'And then it saw me and flicked its tongue . . . and then . . . and then I couldn't move, and I yelled for you and it started moving . . .' She lifted her head and wiped her nose with her hand.

Stride squatted beside her.

'I thought I was going to die,' she gulped. She

sniffed and used her forearm to wipe her eyes. She tried to stand, pushing her hands against the tree for support.

'It's gone, Jess. You scared it away.'

'Oh, God. I can't stand, my legs . . . I . . .' She slid down, her hands trembling. Her nervous laugh threatened to turn to sobs.

'It's okay. You're okay, Jess,' said Stride. 'How did you know I was here?'

'I saw you.' Her voice steadied.

'But I didn't see any other footprints.'

'I found a track through the scrub – the back way. I've been here before, remember. You didn't see me that time either.'

Stride said nothing. He knew of no other track that came in through the back way, but he wasn't going to admit that.

'The snake . . .' she started.

'It's okay – it's more frightened of us than we are of it.'

'I wouldn't be sure of that.' She laughed uncertainly.

Stride knelt down beside her. 'Snakes won't attack unless you threaten them.'

'Yes . . . but . . . I don't think this one was that discriminating.'

Stride smiled. His pulse slowed and the bush smelt familiar again. The noise of the cicadas rose again to a cheerful hum and a breeze lifted, drying the perspiration on the back of his neck.

'Yeah, I saw my first snake out at my gramps's place. It was weird. There's something spooky about them, like they mesmerise you. It's their eyes I think.'

'Yeah, that one kept staring at me like it was challenging me or something.' She paused. 'What if it had bitten me? Was it poisonous?'

'Yep, red-bellied black snake . . . Dangerous all right. Locals would say you should be wearing boots and thick socks through here.'

'You're not.'

'Nah . . . Probably should though.'

Jess closed her eyes for a moment and wrapped her arms around herself.

'I think I've almost stopped shaking now.' She stood and lifted her backpack onto one shoulder. 'That's cured me of coming here alone. Promise you'll come with me next time?'

Stride hesitated. He shifted Ferd onto his wrist. He looked at Jess and half smiled. 'Mmm . . . maybe.'

'It's only because I like Ferd, don't get any ideas.'

Stride shook his head. 'You're unbelievable.'

Jess managed a small smile. '*And* I need someone who knows the terrain.'

'You've been sussing the terrain perfectly well on your own.'

''Cept for today.' She looked up at him and her voice became small. 'You came just at the right time.'

'Coincidence.'

'Whatever it was, I was relieved to see you.'

Stride eyed her silently, unsure.

'You're so . . . so . . .'

'So what?'

'Oh, I dunno . . .'

'Can I carry Ferd?'

Stride sighed. 'And you never give up.'

Another giggle. 'No . . . well, yes, when I've got what I want.'

'Here.' Stride unclipped Ferd and passed him across. He undid the band and fastened it on Jess's wrist. She was watching Ferd, smiling.

'There,' said Stride, 'Now you can't say I'm scared of letting him go.'

'Oh.' For a second Jess frowned. 'I've got a big mouth, haven't I?' She ran her fingers down Ferd's back. Ferd shut his eyes and 'crrked' softly, tamping his tongue on the inside of his beak. She gently lifted one wing, smoothing the yellow feathers.

'Am I really the only one who's ever minded him?'

'I'm starving. Are you?'

She looked at Stride. 'You didn't answer me.'

Stride looked away. 'Well, yes. Usually, people don't want to hold a great big bird. They want to pat him and get him doing dumb tricks and stuff, but they don't ask to hold him.'

'Oh, really?'

'Yeah – you're a bit weird that way.'

'That makes you weird too, then.'

Stride gave a snorty laugh. 'I guess so. But Ferd was my dad's, so . . .' He trailed off.

'Was?'

'Yeah . . . my dad . . . he's . . . he's . . . ah . . . not around.'

'Your parents separated?'

'No.'

'You don't have a dad?'

'Not anymore,' said Stride. 'He died last year.'

'Oh.'

They were out of the scrub now and onto a track. Shortly it swung left and lost definition as it merged into the sand dunes on the Seal Bay side of the lagoon.

'What's your excuse then?' Stride asked.

'For what?'

'For your weirdness?'

'Oh . . . you mean with Ferd?'

'Yeah.'

'Well, it's probably to do with my dad, too. He ran an animal shelter for years so we always had animals in the house and in the yard. I'm pretty comfy with all sorts of furry, feathery things.'

'But not Joe Blakes.'

'Joe Blakes?'

'Joe Blakes – snakes – you know?'

Jess grinned. 'No. I've never heard snakes called Joe Blakes – that is so . . . lame . . . No, I never got comfortable with . . . Joe Blakes.'

At the water's edge, they ambled through the shallows. Small waves washed up to their knees and foam bubbles popped against their calves. Salt dried in the hot sun on their skin making their legs feel tight and shiny.

'So you didn't know about that track we just walked back on?'

'I never said that.'

'Yes, but you let me lead. If you knew it, you'd have led.' She turned and grinned, her eyes bright in the beach glare.

Stride shook his head. 'What is it with you? It's like you're constantly trying to pick a fight.'

'I'm not normally like this. It's just that you . . . you . . . you're so easy to stir.'

'Yeah, well, I'm especially easy to stir right now – I'm ravenous.'

'I'll shout you chips . . . for saving my life.'

'Excessive, but . . . yeah . . . whatever.'

'There you are, Jess. Hello . . . Stride, isn't it?' Jess's father was stretched out on a banana lounge with a book.

'Hi, Dad,' said Jess.

Stride nodded hello as Jess handed Ferd back to him. Ferd squawked and pressed his beak into Stride's shirt pocket. Stride pulled out a handful of seed from his shorts pocket and held it up. Ferd did a dance along Stride's arm, crest up and wings held out a little from his body.

'Oh, Ferd, you're such a show off – but a cute one. Isn't he gorgeous, Dad?'

'He's a wonderful bird. Healthy and strong, too, by the look of him. You obviously take good care of him, Stride.'

Stride smiled and his cheeks reddened slightly.

'We're going to get some lunch, Dad. Can I have some money?'

'Well, there's chicken in the esky.'

'Can we have that for dinner? I'd like to buy Stride lunch.'

'Okay,' said Jock, his eyebrows lifted.

'Stride saved my life, so I owe him.'

'Really?'

'Nah, she didn't need saving. She can look after herself.'

'What happened?'

'I met this huge black snake and it was going to attack me and then Stride ran gallantly in and wrestled it to the ground and strangled it.'

'And who rushed in to rescue the snake?'

'I knew you'd say that, Dad. No concern for your daughter.'

'What was the real story?'

'Oh, boring – I was terrified, and the snake made a quick getaway.'

'So, no wrestling and no strangling?'

'No.'

'Well, I'm pleased you're both okay, but, you know, if you ever have a choice between travelling in a car and confronting a snake, the snake's the safer option.'

'You're so predictable, Dad. I'll travel by snake next time. See you later.'

11 Family

They walked through the shallows again, until a wave soaked Jess's shorts. The same wave made Ferd raise his crest and beat his wings so hard that Stride had to move his head to one side and stretch his arm out away from the flapping wings.

'Ferd would love to fly, wouldn't he?'

'He flies at home. When he's in the house.'

'Yes, but I mean out here, out in the open.'

Stride didn't answer. He ran his hand down Ferd's tail feathers and neither spoke until they reached the surf shop.

'Hey, Dooks,' said Stride.

Dooks was kneeling on the sand cleaning wax off the hire boards.

'Oh, g'day,' he said. 'What are you two up to?'

'Just getting some chips. You busy?'

'Yeah. This wax has been building up for six months, I reckon.'

'Remind Cruso about gorilla grip.'

'Yeah, I'd be out of a job, then.'

Stride shrugged. 'Cruso should have you out there teaching grommets, not cleaning hire boards.'

'I wish. I'm going for my bronze medallion next month. Then he might change his mind – trust me with the kids.'

Stride nodded. 'Yeah. Good luck.'

Dooks turned to Jess. 'Done any surfing?'

Jess smiled and shook her head.

'It's a waste – you walking when you were made to spend your life on a board,' Dooks said.

Stride rolled his eyes. 'Smooth, Dooks.'

Dooks grinned. 'Well, it's true . . . She's a natural.'

Jess looked uncomfortably from one to the other.

'Uh, still starving, Stride?' she said.

'Yeah.'

'Let's go.'

Dooks sat back on his haunches. 'Come and get me when you're going in.'

'Sure,' Stride called.

They climbed the stairs and turned toward the main street.

'Do you want to surf?' asked Jess.

'I always want to surf.'

'With Dooks?'

Stride lifted Ferd onto his shoulder.

'Do you?'

Jess stopped walking, put her head on one side and stroked Ferd's craggy toes where they pressed into Stride's shoulder.

'I'd rather just go with you.'

Stride breathed out and gave a small lopsided smile.

'Good. Later today, maybe?'

Jess nodded and her hand stayed resting on Stride's shoulder, a finger curled under one of Ferd's claws.

At the top of the rise they could see the cluster of shops.

'My sister works in the milk bar.'

'Really? I didn't know you had a sister. Older?'

'Yeah.'

'Do you look alike?'

'Nah, I look like Mum, she's like Dad.'

'What's her name?'

'Annie. I'll get her to make us a milkshake – she makes *the* best milkshakes.'

They ordered chips and sat at a table outdoors where they could see the beach.

'Look, surf's coming up – should be good by about five, I reckon.'

'How do you know?'

'See how the wind has swung around. It was onshore, but it's more northerly now. Did you feel the breeze at our backs down on the beach? I reckon it'll keep swinging around and be offshore by this evening when the tide changes – perfect.'

'I'm impressed. But what's so good about offshore winds?'

'They lift the waves. Onshore winds tend to flatten them.'

Jess was watching Stride.

'You do know your terrain, don't you?'

'What about you? Your surfing was pretty impressive.'

'Well, I have surfed a bit.'

'How much is "a bit"?'

'I went out a few times last summer – that's all. My older brother was a surfer.'

'Your brother's a surfer?'

'Yeah, he was a longboard champion.'

'No way. What, mals?'

'Yeah. He's got about six malibus. We've even got an old twelve footer in the shed – wooden.'

'You're joking.'

'No. He doesn't surf anymore, though. Had a bad fall.'

'So he taught you?'

'Well, not really. I've watched him heaps, and I kind of picked it up. My parents don't want me to surf, though – not after what happened to Justin.'

'Did your dad know you went out the other day?'

'Yeah – he was okay with that.'

'Well, no wonder you're a natural – it's in your blood. But . . . but . . . you let Dooks show you all the moves like you'd never seen a board before.' Stride paused. 'Did you tell Dooks any of this stuff with your brother?'

Jess shrugged. 'Nah. Lots of people in the surfing world have heard of Justin. When he had his accident there were heaps of articles in surfing mags. People criticised him for taking risks – for surfing the dangerous reef breaks. So I don't like talking about it – in case they feel the need to share their opinion. That happened a lot and it was . . .' Jess swallowed and looked away.

'It was brutal.' She rested her chin in her hand. 'So . . . well, I usually don't say anything.'

Stride nodded. 'Right. But you told me?'

Jess smiled. 'I understood you from the moment I saw you striding through the camp site with that great bird on your shoulder.'

Stride reddened. 'And then it was all downhill from there.'

Jess giggled. 'No, not *all* downhill.'

'Oh, hi, Stride. I didn't know you were here.' Annie was at the table with the order of chips.

'Hi,' she said to Jess. 'I'm Annie. Big sister.'

'Annie, this is Jess.'

'Hi, Jess. Are you a camper?'

'Yep – from the foreshore.'

'Cool.'

'I promised Jess one of your milkshakes,' said Stride.

'I do sensational milkshakes. What flavour, Jess? Wait, let me guess. What about a Mocha with double-choc ice-cream?'

'Perfect.'

'Don't know that *you* deserve one after last night's effort,' Annie said to Stride.

'Yeah, I lost it, didn't I? Sorry. I'll have another go and get it right.'

'At least you did the dishes for me.'

Annie sauntered back inside and Stride leaned against his chair.

'What was that about?'

Stride groaned. 'Do I have to go into it?'

'Yes, or I'll nag till you do.'

Stride took a deep breath. 'Well, Mum put our house on the market . . . that's why I was so mad at the real estate agent's office. That's when I found out the house was up for sale. Annie and I are trying to get Mum to change her mind. We don't want to leave. But we have to be diplomatic. Annie's good at it, but I'm a hothead.'

'So last night you lost it?'

'Yep – wasn't pretty.'

Jess nodded.

Ferd wig-wagged across the footpath, dragging his chain which was attached to the rung of Stride's chair. Jess watched him.

'You know what most impressed me about you?'

'Not more "This is Your Life",' Stride said. 'What? My temper tantrum in the street? My temper tantrum when I thought you'd lost Ferd?'

'Nope. Definitely not the temper tantrums. I first saw you with those little horrors – the Morgan kids, who are camped just behind us. You didn't show off or try to get Ferd to perform.'

'No, I just fell over – yeah, very impressive.'

Jess giggled. 'That was pretty funny . . . and then I was a real know-it-all.'

'Yeah you were, weren't you.'

'Yeah, but I didn't know that stuff about sunflower seeds. When I told dad about that, he said I should've, that it was basic.'

'Yeah, he was right.'

'Don't rub it in.'

Stride made a pile of seed for Ferd under the table.

'How come your sister's got a job and you don't?' asked Jess.

'How do you know I don't have one?'

'Well?'

'I'm meant to do all the handyman jobs around the house and get paid for it. But you could say that the system has kind of broken down. Mum and I keep blueing and then I'm too grumpy to fix anything.'

'What else are you fighting about?'

'Oh, just stuff . . . everything . . . and the house being for sale has just made it all worse.'

Annie arrived and placed two milkshakes on the table.

'Thanks,' said Jess.

'Are you surfing this afternoon?' asked Annie.

'We'll probably go down later.'

'We? Do you surf, Jess?'

'Yeah, a bit. Do you?

'No, can't bear all that lugging around. Boards are so clunky. I like to body surf though.'

'When do you knock off?' asked Stride.

'About four.'

'We'll come and get you.'

'Ace.' She turned to go and then stopped, squatting beside Stride. 'If life at home is going to be bearable . . . you know that list of jobs Mum's got taped to the fridge?'

'Yeah, yeah.'

'Stride, if we want convince her not to sell the house, we have to be prepared to put in.'

Stride nodded. 'Yeah – I know.'

Annie wiped the table with a cloth then stacked the dirty cups on the next table and took them inside.

'So you're the man around the house?'

'Supposedly.'

'Pressure, huh?'

'Tell me about it.'

'My mum's on her own, and Justin's in a wheel-chair, so Mum and I do most of the domestic stuff.'

'In a wheelchair? Your brother can't walk?'

'No.'

'The surfing accident?'

'Yes. Dad comes around and helps sometimes. He put ramps and railings up – fixed the house to make it easier for Jus – and us – to manage.'

'Is he a carpenter?'

'No, not really, but he says he'd do anything for Jus . . .'

Suddenly, unexpectedly, Stride felt a lump in his throat. He pictured his mum and the growing list on the fridge at home; Mum wanting to get the house spruced up for sale; Gramps on his own at the farm; and he thought of his dad, coming home, just sometimes to help out, like Jess's dad . . . His longing was so strong, the pain so overwhelming, he almost felt crippled by it.

He stood up hurriedly, unclipping Ferd's chain from the chair rung. 'I've got to go. I'll come and get you when the tide turns.'

Jess frowned, looking up at him. 'But . . . What about your milkshake?'

'You have it.' He lifted Ferd onto his shoulder and strode away.

12 Fire

Stride sat on the front step and picked at the peeling paint on the wall beside him. The dash home had stilled him and he wished he was back drinking his chocolate milkshake with Jess. He should have told her how he felt. He owed it to her after she had been so honest. He kicked at the path, sending gravel flying onto the lawn.

Ferd squawked and flew to the full extent of his chain. Stride eased him back down onto his wrist, calmed him, then ducked into the shed. He emerged with a piece of rope. He attached it to Ferd's chain, tripling the length of it.

'Go on, mate – have a go,' Stride murmured.

Ferd tilted his head to one side, 'crrked' and his eyes followed Stride's pointed finger to the roof of the house. He spread his wings, rose effortlessly and landed on the corrugated iron. He stared down at Stride, eyes bright and crest up, and then one foot after another, he walked along the rusty guttering. He dipped his head forward and came up with a pine cone in his beak, then proceeded to pull it apart, making contented 'crrking' sounds.

Stride smiled. 'Silly bird,' he muttered. 'Got a good view from up there?'

Ferd tore at the cone, raining pine cone chunks down onto Stride. Stride shielded his eyes against the sun and falling debris. From here, he couldn't see the ring on Ferd's leg, or the chain. Ferd looked as free as one of the cockatoos in the small flocks of wild birds that sometimes roosted in the pine tree.

Ferd's feathers ruffled as the northerly gusted through the tree and across the roof. He lifted his head, cocking it one side and then the other, watching the sky.

Stride turned and a sharp scent filled his nostrils. Then he saw it: a thin spiral of smoke rising in the sky to the north-west. He hurried around the house to get a better look. Who would burn off on a day like today? It was madness. No one. No one would burn off on a day like today.

As he watched, the smoke changed colour and shape. It became dark blooms growing higher against the blue. Stride stood, transfixed by the dark stain sprawling across the sky, the smell gaining strength.

'Ferd! Quick!' Stride pulled on the rope. Ferd squawked, nearly overbalanced, raised his crest, glared, then turned back to demolishing his second pine cone.

'Ferd! Come down!' Stride scrabbled in his pocket for seed. Ferd ignored him.

'You stupid bird – you've got to come down now!'

Ferd hesitated for another moment, dropped the cone and half jumped, half flew to Stride's outstretched arm. With his free hand, Stride fumbled with the rope. His hands shook and the sun felt hot on the back of his neck. He quickly re-attached the chain.

Inside, he unclipped Ferd's chain and raced for the phone. He started to dial. Who was he dialling? He replaced the receiver.

The front door slammed. Footsteps.

Annie stood in the doorway. She bent forward, her head against the door jamb, her hands holding onto the door handle.

'Oh you're here – thank God. There's a fire. It's close.'

'I saw it. What . . . what are you doing here?'

'Simone's closing the shop, so she let me go. I came to find you, and I'm worried about Mum.'

'She's at work, isn't she?'

'Yes, but what if she needs to get home? Bernie from the CFA called in to the shop and apparently campers inland from Point Wondai lit a campfire. The CFA is worried by this wind. There're five trucks on their way.'

'How far away is it?'

'Not sure, but it's heading towards Seal Bay.'

Annie dialled.

'Mum? Have you heard any news? Can you see the smoke? Yes. I'm at home and I can see it through the window.'

Stride pushed aside the blind. All he could see was smoke.

'It's moving fast . . . Yes, he's okay, he's here . . . What are you going to do? . . . Bernie says the coast road from Point Wondai isn't safe, and the river road inland will probably be blocked off . . . Okay . . . be careful . . . Yes, I'll tell him . . . See you soon.'

'What's she doing?'

'She's going to try to get back. She said to say she loves you – and me.'

They stood together at the window, watching as the sky turned darker. The great billowing cloud was tinged orange, and the horizon glowed red.

Annie took Stride's arm. She was shaking. 'What should we do?'

'I'm not sure.' He slipped his hand onto her shoulder, squeezing it to steady his hand. 'What about Gramps?'

Annie covered her mouth. 'When Mum comes, we'll go and get him.'

Stride swallowed. He said nothing, but he knew it would be too late by then. He scrambled for the phone.

'He's not answering.' His voice was high pitched and unsteady.

'Ring the CFA.'

Stride dialled.

'This is Stride Walker . . . Yes . . . Seal Bay . . . I'm worried about my grandfather. He lives alone on the inland road . . . Yes . . . South . . . No, RMB 1256. Yes, James Walker . . . No, my mum's not here . . . How long? . . . Okay . . . Yes . . . Yes . . . Thanks.'

'What can they do?'

'They'll try to send someone out there.'

'When?'

'As soon as they can . . . What's that noise?'

A vehicle was coming along the track to their drive-way. It had the clatter of a diesel motor in low gear and a loudspeaker crackled above the sound of the engine.

'. . . take water, food and blankets with you. All residents – we are calling all residents to put their fire plan into action. Please do not panic, but act without delay. If you are leaving, please take water, food and blankets with you. All residents . . .'

Annie's chin trembled. 'Fire plan? What fire plan?'

Stride stood still, his heart pounding. He breathed deeply and willed his heart to slow down as he wiped his damp palms down his thighs. 'We'll go to the beach. Remember at school when we did fire drill and they said we should meet at the letterbox? I was worried because we don't have a letterbox, so I asked Dad. He said, "Bugger the letterbox, get yourself down to the beach quick smart."'

Annie's mouth softened. She brushed the tears off her cheeks.

'Yeah, I remember that . . . Just like dad.' And her voice broke.

'Grab a woollen blanket. I'll get water.'

He shoved water bottles, biscuits, cheese, fruit and birdseed into a bag. Ferd, watching from his post on top of Stride's door, flew down to the bench.

'Good boy, Ferd,' said Stride and clicked on his chain, lifting him onto his shoulder. Annie pressed blankets on top of the bag.

'I'll tell Mum what we're doing.' Annie picked up the phone. 'Myra? Is Mum there? . . . Oh. Which way did she go? . . . Okay, I'll try her mobile, thanks.' She hung up and dialled again.

'She's not answering.'

'Come on, we'll leave her a note.'

Halfway to the ti-tree tunnel, Annie yelled, 'Stride, wait!' She put down her load and ran back.

Stride stared at the little square house with its crumbling render, the patchy whitewash, the short eaves, the brick chimney and the huge pine tree rising behind it. Beyond that rose a huge pall of smoke that overshadowed the whole western sky, tinting everything orange. Wind blew in fierce erratic gusts. The ti-trees were bent double and dry leaves skittered down the path to the sand.

Ferd squawked, his eyes wide. His crest was forward and he tipped his head to one side, eyeing the sky as the wind funnelled lines between his feathers revealing blue scaly skin.

The door slammed and Annie was panting beside him. In her bag were the family photo albums, their mother's watercolour paints and brushes and Annie's flute.

Stride dropped his bag and raced back inside, with Ferd scrambling to keep balance on his shoulder. In his room he scrabbled in the back of his wardrobe. He grabbed his father's Bluey, and pulling the door shut behind him, raced outside. Together they ran down the tunnel through the deepening gloom to the beach.

In the camping ground, the campers were in a frenzy of packing. They grabbed belongings and stuffed them into bags and boxes. Clotheslines hung with towels, bathers, wetsuits and socks were hurled, pell mell, into car boots. There was yelling, confusion and running and persuading and screaming and shushing and crying and reassuring and car doors slamming. At the southern end of the beach, Seal Bay residents were streaming down the steps, lugging children, bags and bedding.

Just above the high tide line, where the sand was dry, Stride and Annie made a small pile of belongings and watched the smoke edge closer.

'My bike! Here, hold Ferd, I've got to get my bike!'

'Stride, you don't need your bike. Don't go back.'

'I do need it.' He unclipped Ferd, pressed the chain and band into Annie's hand.

'Here.' She pushed the Bluey into his hands, 'Take this . . .'

He dodged trailers, sagging tarpaulins, ropes and tent pegs to the path. Black flakes of ash swirled in the wind, and the scent of fire was strong in the air. The sun became a huge orange yolk suspended in the smoke, then disappeared altogether. It was getting darker and a low roar underpinned the tearing wind.

The white walls of the house stood stark against the howling backdrop. Smoke stung Stride's eyes and nose. Around the side of the house a wall of heat blasted his bare legs and arms as he turned the corner. For a moment he stopped, unsure whether he should stop or keep going. He thought of Gramps – the long uncut grass, the tinder-dry weatherboards, the derelict Holden, the explosive haze of eucalypt oil hovering in the air . . . The dark and dripping dugout carved into the hillock behind Gramps's house where he and Annie used to play as kids. It had collapsed during a winter storm last year. The quick hug, the pulling away . . . He must get his bike.

He slipped the Bluey over his head and ran for the shed. The metal latch was hot to touch. He pulled his arm up into the sleeve, and knocked the latch back, once, twice, three times. It clicked and Stride wrenched the door. He grabbed the bike and pushed it outside. Orange tongues of fire licked towards the roof of the house from the pine tree. A sheet of flame shot up with a roar, sending sparks skyward.

He mounted the bike and frantically pumped the pedals. The bike shot forward, skidding and snaking on the grass. Then Stride was in the tunnel, leaping over tree roots, whipped by the turbulence at his back. The front tyre hit the soft sand and he was nearly pitched over the handlebars. He dismounted and ran, dodging the disarray in the camping ground, dragging the bike behind him.

On the beach, Annie was standing knee-deep in the shallows, stepping over the lapping waves, her face streaming, a wet blanket around her, Ferd on her shoulder and the family albums in her arms. Stride dropped the bike on the sand and waded in, taking Ferd.

'Stride!' She yelled. 'Look . . . the house . . . look at the house . . .' But the wind swamped the words.

Stride and Annie stood together in the sea and watched as burning branches fell from the pine tree onto the roof. Eager flames flickered and died and rose again, then gradually joined together until the house was engulfed and became a mass of fire, crackling and roaring, sending great shafts of flame and black smoke into the air. Holes in the roof yawned into chasms and sheets of iron loosened and slipped inward or were flung on boiling air to land in treetops and on the embankment. Fire greedily devoured the wooden shed, the flames feeding noisily on its contents.

Annie covered her mouth with her hand and dropped to her knees, losing her grip on the albums. Stride bent down, but wasn't quick enough. Loose photos spiralled down in slow motion to the water. They turned and watched images of a young chubby Stride, a shy slender Annie, a youthful dark-haired Frank and a tall laughing Caroline, slide beneath the white foam that washed them up the beach and then tugged them gently back out again.

Stride and Annie lunged, grabbed and lunged again, as they struggled to see through the blur of tears. Little squares of colour bobbed and ebbed on the waves, holding the history of their family as the rest of it turned to ash up on the hill.

13 The Farm

Stride stared up at the smoking ruin, the brick chimney rising dark against the sky. All along Seal Bay the silhouette was unfamiliar. Where there had been houses, there were now blackened holes, like rotted teeth. Bushland had become burned skeletons, trunks smouldering, burning to the core.

The fire had finished its work here, but further south the great mass of roiling smoke continued unabated.

Annie spread the rug on the beach in a sheltered hollow in the dune.

'Will you be all right here by yourself?' Stride put his hand on Annie's shoulder. Her face was turned seaward, but it seemed to Stride, she saw nothing.

She didn't answer.

'I reckon Mum'll be here soon, and I have to find out if Gramps is okay.'

Annie sat with the albums pressed against her chest, a little pile of warped photos on her lap.

'Annie?'

'Just go,' she said finally. 'Of course you have to.' Stride tried to put his arm around her, but she pushed him away. 'Go . . . don't ask me if it's okay . . . of course it's not . . . but it has to be done . . . just go. I'll wait for Mum.'

Stride stood, clipped Ferd to the handlebars and tucked the Bluey onto the back of his bike.

At the end of the beach, the surf shop was untouched. Alongside the shop, the CFA had erected a huge tarpaulin. They were providing drinks and food. People were milling around, lugging belongings uncertainly. Children were subdued, lost in their parents' confusion.

At the stairs, he half carried, half pushed his bike up the steps. Almost at the top, he bumped the front tyre and Ferd lurched forward, squawking and flapping his wings, his crest up.

'Do you want a hand – someone to carry the bird, maybe?'

He looked over his shoulder. 'Jess!'

'Isn't this awful! Are you okay, Stride?'

'Jess, I can't stop. Can you take Ferd for a moment? That would be brilliant.'

She unclipped him, and Stride dragged his bike to the top of the stairs.

'Where are you going?'

'I've got to find out if my Gramps is okay.'

'But . . . but . . . you've only got a bike and it's a bushfire, Stride!'

'I know, but I've got to do this.' Stride took Ferd, re-clipped him to the handlebars and swung his leg across the saddle.

'You can't go alone.'

'Well I am.'

'Well, then – I'm coming.'

Jess hitched her leg across the coat on the packrack, standing on either side of the bike on tip-toes.

Stride stared at her. 'You can't come – it's too hard.'

'What do you mean? I won't let you go alone.'

'Jess I'm not arguing . . . your dad . . .'

'Dad's helping the CFA. Quick, how far is it to your gramps's place.'

Stride grasped the handlebars and pushed off, pressing down hard. Jess grabbed his shoulders.

'Too far! This is madness,' he yelled over his shoulder. 'We'll never get through. There'll be road-blocks and police.'

'Desperate times call for desperate measures,' she yelled against the rush of air.

Through the town, Stride could see where the fire had veered west and turned inland at the main road. On this side trees glistened, their leaves green and their trunks untouched while tall grasses, their seeding heads intact, bowed in the breeze.

'Why did you run off from the milk bar this morning?' Jess yelled. Her hands were knotted into the sides of his T-shirt.

'Sorry' Stride called back, 'I'll explain – but not now.'

He felt Jess relax against him and he pedalled hard. The landscape was a black and white ruin and the air was thick with smoke and the death stink of it. The road ran a ghostly ribbon through the silent remnants of the forest, free of bird call and insect noise. Some trees were singed, others green at the top, blackened to the waist, or completely burnt, their brown leaves hanging forlornly.

Exposed on the bare ground were fallen logs, blackened bottles and cans, and smoking mounds puffed like earth ovens. Animal pathways that had been tunnelled through grass and ferns were gone, shelters were laid open, burrows and hollows lay exposed. Tree stumps glowed and large trees oozed smoke.

The fire had travelled fast. By now, it must have reached the farm. Had the CFA got there? Stride tried not to think about it.

He couldn't tell how far they were from the fire, but the wind was fierce at their back, hurtling them, and the fire front ahead of them, south. Jess had her arms tight around him, her face sheltered behind his back. Ferd's feathers were grey with ash, his beak wide, and his crest high. As they got closer, the fire-generated wind skittered ash across the road, and rattled the crisp leaves above them. It grew darker and the smell of the burning forest was more eucalyptus and smoke, less charcoal. With every corner Stride expected to be turned back. But the fire was tearing faster than they could ride.

Stride ignored his jelly-legs and parched throat, too dry to swallow. He wished he'd brought the water from the bag on the beach. His chest burned and the pain in his calves felt like knife wounds. He pedalled faster than he'd ever pedalled before and they took the final bend at a speed that almost toppled them.

There was the old gate. It was twisted beyond recognition, the grass on either side blackened to ash. The vegetable patch was gone, the chook pen decimated.

Stride's heart pumped and perspiration dripped off his chin onto his wet shirt. His swollen tongue had all moisture sucked from it. His eyes streamed, making pink trails through the dirt down the side of his face.

They had no view of the house yet, but suddenly there was an explosion followed by another and another and a column of black smoke shot above the burning tree stumps.

Stride skidded to a halt. Ferd squawked and once more nearly overbalanced, rose and flapped wildly in the air. Jess leaped off and reached up for Ferd. Stride felt as though his hands were glued to the handlebars. His legs had no strength and almost gave way as he tried to stand.

'Stay here.' His voice cracked like a dry twig. He thrust the bike at Jess, slipping on the sleeves of the Bluey as he ran.

Around the curve of the driveway, Stride stopped. The farmhouse was alight.

'Nooo–' The word was torn away in the burning air. 'Gramps! Gramps!'

He raced forward, pulling the Bluey over his head. But the fire roared and the heat stung his flesh. Each time he tried to get near, he was thrust back.

The house was backlit by a mass of flame. The roof was buckling and twisting like a wild animal trying to escape, until, finally sheet after sheet lifted gracefully and cartwheeled into the garden.

The dark front door frame distorted and gave in, falling backward. Flames spouted from the windows and the roof fell too. Then as if in slow motion, the verandah disintegrated, followed by the front wall and finally the whole house collapsed.

Embers shot high in the air, spraying ash and sparks. Suddenly Stride felt heat on his back. The Bluey had caught alight. He flailed at it with his hands, fell to the ground and rolled madly on the dirt. He pulled it off and hurled it away, feeling a tug at the armband on his wrist as he did so.

There was a WHOOF behind him. The Holden erupted in a ball of fire. Flames gusted high into the air, black smoke mushroomed above them. Stride's legs gave way and he dropped to his knees. He tried to crawl away from the furnace, his chest heaving.

'Stride!' The scream rose above the chaos. He

clambered to his feet, coughing, his nose streaming, his eyes barely able to see.

'Stride!' It was Jess. He struggled towards her, wheezing and bent low.

Jess was squatting on the ground, her face white. 'I can't calm him. He won't let me . . . there's something wrong.'

Ferd was on the ground, his wings spread out on the dirt, his eyes wide, his beak open in a silent screech. His crest was frozen upright and his claws were clenched shut.

'Ferd!' Stride knelt down beside him and tried to lift him. Ferd thrashed his wings, beating against Stride, Jess and the ground.

'What can we do?' Jess's knuckles were white.

Stride couldn't hear the fire anymore. Couldn't smell the smoke or feel the pain in his lungs. He lifted Ferd gently on to his lap. 'It's all right, Ferd. It's all right.' He smoothed Ferd's ruffled wings and crest and stroked his back, easing his claws until they curled around Stride's wrist.

'There's nothing to be afraid of, old boy,' he murmured. He turned to Jess, 'Unclip him, Jess.'

She stood and stared at Stride, her mouth open. 'But . . .'

'Please. Just do it, Jess.' Stride's voice was a whisper.

She knelt and released the clip. Stride got to his feet and lifted Ferd above his head, making soothing sounds as he did.

'It's okay, Ferd . . . you're free to go.'

Ferd crouched for a second on Stride's outstretched hand. Then he tilted his head, raised his wings, and screeched as he lifted into the air, cleared the wetland and was swallowed by the smoke.

They stood together, Jess's hand on Stride's arm.

'Stride . . . you . . . you let him go.'

Stride didn't answer. He wiped a sleeve across his face and squatted in the dirt, his head between his knees.

14 Refuge

Beyond the farm, the pall of smoke was inching south. The roar had retreated, the wind gusts were less frequent. Jess sat beside Stride staring at the grey remains of Gramps's house. Burnt timber beams leaned at precarious angles; occasional hisses and pops sent ash swirling in chalky eddies.

Stride felt like his chest had caved in. His head pounded, his lips were cracked and he could only just see through his swelling eyes.

'I need water.' His voice was barely audible. 'Let's go to the dam.'

They followed the downward course of the dry waterway. Here the fire had skirted the foliage and there was a hint of the familiar scent of bush mint. Just beneath that, Stride could sense the earthy smell of the dam. He started to run. He could see the slender gum on the far side of the bank above the regrowth – its trunk white, the long strings of bark intact and its leaves green.

He burst through the ring of thick bushes skirting the dam. The water was silent and dark, untroubled. There, on the opposite bank was . . . What was it? Stride halted, holding his hands to his painful eyes. He blinked. A white shape wig-wagged over the mud. It bent low to drink, dropping back its head to let the water run down its throat. Then another movement – beside him. Stride squinted into the gloom.

'What is it, Stride?' Jess pressed behind him.

Stride surged around the dam towards the figure on the bank. Beside it, huddled in the shallows, were two grey roos licking their wet fur, their ears twitching. Circling, in the centre of the dam, was a family of wood ducks, heads cocked at the sky.

The roos saw the two intruders and, streaming muddy water, bounded into the narrow neck of remaining bush, the thump of their tails resounding through the scorched earth. The ducks eyed the newcomers and slid across the surface, merging into the reeds on the other side.

Stride scrambled along the bank, sliding on the wet clay, falling to his knees, getting up, slipping again and splashing through the shallows.

'Gramps!' His voice cracked. He was on his knees, his arms out. 'Gramps!' He took hold of the bowed damp figure on the bank and hugged hard. 'Gramps! Gramps! I thought . . . I thought . . . the fire . . .' He paused, words tripping over each other. 'The farmhouse is gone and I was so . . . scared . . . so sure that you . . .' he trailed off, his voice lost in the painful lump in his throat.

'Diggy, Diggy . . . it's all right. I'm all right.'

Stride let go and sank onto the clay bank, staring at Gramps, shaking his head, his eyes stinging all over again. Gramps's clothes were sodden and water dripped from his hat making a brown stain on his shoulders. He reached out and took Stride's hand.

'I knew you were here when Ferd flew in,' Gramps said. Ferd flung his crest forward, screeched, and half hopped, half flew to land on Stride's knees. He bobbed up and down, then swung up until he was hanging from Stride's shirt by his beak. Gramps gently stroked his crest. 'He's been drinking non-stop.'

Stride nodded and grinned stupidly, lifting Ferd on his hand and pressing his nose against the grubby feathers below Ferd's eye. Ferd blinked and settled low on Stride's fist.

Stride splashed water over his face, then drank, letting water run down his chest and back. Jess, beside him, lay on her stomach and drank too.

'Diggy – your friend?'

Jess sat up, wiping her mouth.

'This is Jess. Jess, this is Gramps.'

'Yeah, I guessed that.' She smiled at Gramps and grabbed his hand, squeezing it for a moment. 'I'm pleased to meet you.' Jess's eyes were bright as she gazed at the old man.

Gramps nodded and smiled. He coughed and his breath laboured for a moment.

He glanced at the smoke-filled sky. 'Well, that fire won't be back in a hurry.'

'No.' Stride breathed deeply as he caressed Ferd's chest.

'Crrk.' Ferd clambered onto Stride's lap, where beak over claw, he made his way up to Stride's shoulder. Stride grinned and turned to Jess who ran her fingers down between Ferd's wings.

'Gramps, you haven't got a singed hair on your head!'

'No.' Gramps chuckled quietly. He paused, and a

strange expression crossed his face. 'I knew there was something wrong this morning – I couldn't put my finger on it – but I felt unsettled with that northerly . . . Anyway, when I took the rubbish out, the leaves of the gums along the driveway were darting like a school of frenzied fish. Then the cicadas went silent and the birds – not a sound to be heard. I knew then that, for sure, something was up.

'I tried to ring your place, but there was no dial tone. And then I saw that bloomin' great cloud to the north and I knew we were in for it. By the time I went inside and got the keys to the car, the light had already changed . . . that apricot tinge to it – nasty.

'And then when I tried to start the car, do you think I could get the bloomin' thing going? Fired a couple of times and died. And all the while that cloud getting bigger and bigger in front of me. I tell you, I didn't know what I was going to do.

'You know your dad was always at me to get a mobile phone or some such thing, and I thought it might be a good idea, but of course, never got around to it.

'Anyway, blow me down, if someone doesn't appear at the driver's window. For a moment there, I couldn't figure out who she was, me mind being so addled as it was. All I knew was that she wanted me to get out of the car. So I got out and followed her.

'She kept turning to see if I was still behind her, kept smiling at me. Come to think of it, she didn't speak, not once. And yet, I knew exactly what she was thinking and she knew exactly what I was thinking.

'Once I reached out to her, but she kept just ahead of me. And that was all right – just as it was meant to be . . .

'She had a long plait, right down her back to her waist. You wouldn't have remembered that, Diggy – she had her hair cut long before you were born. I used to plait it for her when we were first married – in winter by the kitchen window, in summer on the verandah.

'And she was wearing the dress I liked on her best of all – the pale blue one, buttons down the back. It was the dress she was wearing when Frank brought the cockatoo chick home all those years ago. She held the little thing against her, didn't care if she got mucky. She tried to feed the little fella, but Frank wouldn't have a bar of it. "I want to raise it, Mum." And he did. Strong-minded he was, your father . . . he was a good boy – Frank. A lot like you, Diggy – strong-willed, but brave.' He looked at Stride intently for a moment, then his eyes drifted and he went on.

'Her feet were bare. I liked that, seeing her so young and carefree. Sometimes I thought she was laughing, but there was no sound that I can recall.

'She led me all the way down here. You know she hadn't been to the dam for ever so long – ten years maybe, and yet she knew the way, hadn't forgotten after all this time.

'We used to swim together here – used to bring your dad and Lenny. We made a raft and the boys used to dive off it. And then you and Annie used to come down . . .'

Gramps stopped talking and looked across the dam.

'What happened then, Gramps?'

'Oh, yes. It was very hot, so I took off my shoes and socks and waded in. She was watching from the bank over there, and smiling. She used to often watch me swim. "Water's your element, Jim," she used to say.

'And then the smoke started to get to me, so I got right in the water, and I felt better . . .

'I could see her silhouette through the water, standing by the sapling. I was real happy she was there. It just felt like old times – you know what I mean, like we'd turned the clock back.

'And then . . . and then . . .' Gramps stopped and looked confused.

151

'What then, Gramps?'

'Well, when I came up, I couldn't see her anymore. She was gone.' He shook his head. 'Do you think . . .' He paused. 'Do you think she's still here? Did you see her?'

Stride took the old man's hand. 'No, Gramps, I didn't see her.'

'No, no, of course not. Well, after that, the fire really heated up and I had to leave my hat on and breathe down close to the water, keeping my clothes wet. By golly, it was hot. And then blow me down, if the roos didn't come up out of the bush, and then the ducks – we were quite a family. And then, the next thing, Ferd flies in. Flew straight to me he did. Didn't you, old fella?'

Ferd lifted his head, 'crrked', and went back to cracking corn.

The four of them sat in silence as the light around them started to fade.

'So, you didn't see the Whoompla, then Gramps?' asked Stride.

Gramps smiled. 'Just seems like yesterday, doesn't it?' He paused. 'Lucky for me, there was no Whoompla today.'

Stride grinned.

Jess stood, looking back towards the house. 'I can hear a vehicle.'

'About time,' muttered Stride. 'Lucky we weren't depending on getting help, eh, Gramps?'

Gramps chuckled. 'All's well that ends well.'

Stride breathed out. 'Yeah, guess so.'

'I'll let them know where we are,' Jess said.

'Okay. We'll start making our way up.' Stride turned to help Gramps to his feet. 'We'd better get back to Seal Bay – can't sleep here tonight.'

'You know, I heard the house go up – saw a shot of black smoke and knew the old place was done for.'

Stride squeezed Gramps's shoulder. 'What's that in your shirt, Gramps?'

'Oh,' Gramps gave a slow smile. 'I picked it up off the mantlepiece when I left the house – I suppose it's all I own now.'

Tucked inside Gramps shirt was a photo of Gran – she was young and wearing a pale blue dress, her hair plaited to her waist and her feet bare.

15 Safe

It was almost dark by the time they got to the two CFA trucks parked by the remnants of Gramps's house, and pitch dark by the time they headed off down the track.

Stride and Jess were squashed in the back of one old fire truck, Gramps in the other. The crackle of the radio drowned out the night and the smell of diesel and stale tobacco mingled with the stench of burned forest.

'This feels . . . safe, solid doesn't it,' murmured Jess.

Stride nodded and slid his free arm along the back of the seat. Jess leaned against him and Stride felt her hair against his arm.

'That conversation we started on the bike . . .' whispered Jess.

'What conversation?'

'The one about you running off this morning leaving me to drink two milkshakes.'

'Was that this morning? It seems like days ago.'

'Don't change the subject.'

'You're like a bull-terrier – once you get a hold of something, you never give up, do you?'

She pulled his hand into her mouth and bit into his finger. 'Never,' she said.

'Okay, okay.'

She let go. 'I thought I must have upset you again, like I did in your shed that day – about letting Ferd go.'

'Nah, it wasn't anything like that. It was just that . . . well . . . when you said your dad sometimes comes home to help, I thought how fantastic it would be to have my dad stroll in the door, how much I'd love him to face that list of Mum's with me, how great it would be to know he was around.'

'Oh.'

'And I thought I was going to blub about it. So instead of embarrassing myself, I ran away.'

'Oh,' she said again. 'I appreciate you telling me.'

'I regretted it as soon as I got home. I kept thinking, why didn't I tell you? You'd been so honest with me. *And*, it was such a waste leaving that milkshake.'

'Of course. That most of all.'

Stride stared at the road. 'And I thought about your brother stuck in a wheelchair, not able to do the thing he loves most, and all I could think about was my own sad little life. While I was watching Gramps's house burn, I kept thinking I should have done more for Gramps, instead of running away, leaving him in his falling-down house with just his useless old car.'

Stride felt Jess's eyes on him in the dark and he relaxed against her. The truck jolted along the track, the lights see-sawing across the alien landscape. Stride closed his eyes, smelt the smoke in Jess's hair, felt the warmth of her seep into him.

They came to the final straight towards Seal Bay where they could see the glow of the lights around the makeshift evacuation centre. The trucks parked up by the CFA shelter where the thump of the generator reverberated through the dark. Light shone through the windscreen, turning Jess's hair silver.

People surged around the trucks, doors slammed and someone hammered on their window, 'Hey – Stride! Jess!'

Stride looked down at Jess. She glanced up and started to speak, changed her mind and their mouths met, hard and clumsy, and his belly flopped like a stranded fish.

'Come on, you two.'

The door was pulled open and Stride, Jess and Ferd slid to the ground, Ferd screeching. Stride raised a hand to calm him and in the other, he held Jess's tightly.

Then Annie was beside him, her arms around his waist, and his mum, crying, her hair slipping out of the clip, her hands on his face.

'Stride . . . you're safe . . . thank God.'

Stride took her hand in his.

'I'm so sorry, for everything . . .' she began.

'No, I'm sorry, Mum.'

16 Home

The sand washed up pink on the shoreline. Clouds hurried south as lines of rain trailed seaward. The sea darkened to a thousand hues of blue, green and grey. Breakers snapped into white lines, racing to shore to be drawn back with a hiss. Seagulls wheeled against the grey sky and a single crow cawed above the treeline as the breeze lifted its ragged silhouette high above the destroyed forest.

There were no surfers today even though regular sets barrelled toward shore. Wind harried the few remaining tents, flapping canvas, lifting doors and window flaps and slapping them back down. A solitary camper in tracksuit pants and thongs bucketed water over a sooty car and broomed a grimy tent wall.

Stride and Jess sat on the knoll where the ti-tree tunnel used to wind down to the beach, their view to the sea now unhindered. A cool breeze riffled Stride's hair and pulled at his T-shirt . . . his only T-shirt. High above them on the blackened pine tree, Ferd sat, preening his feathers and 'crrking' occasionally.

'You really heading home today?' Stride rested his head on Jess's shoulder, pushing her dreadloacks to one side.

'Yeah, we're all packed.'

'What about next holidays?'

'Don't know that I'll be able to talk Dad into another holiday quite like this one.'

'You've got to. You can stay in our brand new house.'

'So your mum's not going to sell?'

'I think her words were: "I can't sell – not the best piece of real estate in Seal Bay."'

'That's brilliant.'

Stride grinned and nodded.

'What made her change her mind?'

'She said, when she was sitting at the roadblock yesterday, not knowing where we were, not knowing if Gramps was safe, or if our house was still there, all she could think about were the fights we'd had. And suddenly, all her reasons for wanting to sell seemed unimportant. She said that the only thing that mattered was that the family was all safely together, no matter where that was . . .' Stride trailed off, a smile curving the corners of his mouth.

Jess watched him for a while without speaking.

'You know, I don't think that smile has left your face all morning.'

Stride chuckled. 'And you know what else? Gramps is going to be living with us . . . I won't have to race out to the farm anymore, scared that something awful's happened to him.'

'That wasn't such a bad thing – it was the best dink I've ever had.'

'It's the only one you'll ever get with me. It did me in, totally – I could hardly stand up.'

'You never know – we might be called on another desperate mission to save a life . . . I think we work quite well as a team.'

'If I remember correctly, we didn't save any lives.'

'Don't be so unheroic – we were in the right place at the right time.'

'Whatever . . . What did your dad say when you got back?'

'Mmm, wasn't that pleased, but I just said, "I'm safe – what else matters?" It works every time. He's such a softy.'

'Where is he now?'

'He's making some calls. He'll be here to pick me up soon.'

They watched the rain moving farther out to sea. The lone camper had finished packing his car. The tide was going out, and rivulets of water furrowed down the beach, pleating the sand into repeated patterns all the way to the water's edge.

'Did I tell you about the house design?'

'No . . . tell.'

'Well, Annie and I have decided Gramps's room will face north-east, my room will have a view of the waves, until the ti-trees grow too high, Annie's plans for her room are extravagant beyond belief and not worth talking about, and Mum's pushing for a painting studio on the south side.' Stride paused. 'Funny, but Mum said for the first time ever, she wants to paint the sea from this spot.'

'Yeah, I'll have to come and check out your mum's paintings . . . and your new house.'

'There's always the bus . . .'

Jess leaned against Stride. Stride pulled a handful of

seed from his pocket with one hand, and put his other arm around Jess.

'Hey, Ferd!'

Ferd squawked and lifted off, gliding down, tilting his wings at the last moment to land on Stride's outstretched arm.

'Stride! Your wristband?'

Stride gazed at the white strip of skin on his left wrist. 'Yeah . . . it's gone.'

'Where?'

'At Gramps's: the Bluey and the armband.'

'Are you going to get them?'

Stride hesitated and lowered his arm, while Ferd pigeon-toed up to his shoulder. 'No, I don't reckon I need to.'

A slow smile spread on Jess's face. 'I knew it – from the very first moment I saw you – I knew you could do it.'

'Do what?' Stride was frowning.

She stroked Ferd's wing. 'Knew you could let him go – and that he'd stay with you anyway.'

Stride shook his head. 'You're crazy . . . you know that?'

She gave her throaty laugh and pushed him.

'You like me that way.'

'Okay . . . you're right this time . . . but it's the only time . . . '

She giggled again and ran her fingers through Ferd's feathers. 'Hey, come here, Ferd.' He blinked at her, twirling a sunflower seed on his beak and wig-wagged over to her, 'crkking' softly. 'You're one lucky bird . . . you know that?' she murmured.

He dropped the husk on her lap, threw his crest forward and danced up and down, lifting his wings slightly from his body.

'You old show-off. You going to be here when I come back?' She slid her finger under his wings. 'Course you are – you know where home is.'

'Yeah.' Stride grinned. 'I guess we all do now.'

JENNI OVEREND is the author of four previous books including *Hello Baby*, illustrated by Julie Vivas, which was short-listed for the 2000 Children's Book Council of Australia awards and selected for the White Ravens collection for the International Youth Library in Munich. Her first book, *Princess Grandma*, won Australia's Multicultural Picture Book of the Year in 1995. Jenni lives in a small mountain township with her husband and four children. She teaches at a little school of eleven children and runs writing classes for adults in the Yarra Valley.

Acknowledgments

My gratitude for the wisdom and support of Chris, Tess, Sunni, Bryn, Bede, Aggie and Julie. For the expertise of Denise Friedman, John Middleton and Ryan Hodges. And to Erica and Jodie for their unending patience and extraordinary faith.